TRACING
THE
Rainbow

ANN GAYLIA O'BARR

Published by Redemption Press Express, an imprint of Redemption Press, PO Box 427, Enumclaw, WA 98022, (360) 226-3488.

Redemption Press Express is honored to present this title in partnership with the author. The views expressed or implied in this work are those of the author. Redemption Press Express provides our imprint seal representing design excellence, creative content, and high-quality production.

All Scripture quotations in this publication are taken from the King James Version of the Bible, public domain.

All lexicon information associated with *Strong's Concordance* was provided by www.blueletterbible.org.

ISBN 13: 978-1-64645-163-0 (Paperback)
978-1-64645-164-7 (ePUB)

Library of Congress Catalog Card Number: 2023912590

TRACING

— THE —

Rainbow

CHAPTER ONE

Montreal, Quebec, Canada
August 1988

*M*ark Pacer enjoyed his job as the American consul in Montreal. And he loved his seven-year-old twins. But he had to admit how much easier a romantic relationship would be if he were simply a single male with a normal job.

His first attempt at a date, arranged by a friend almost two years after Reye died, had resurrected old adolescent doubts and uncertainties.

He arrived at the restaurant early and seated himself at the reserved table on the outdoor sidewalk, perfect for the late-summer evening. He tried to concentrate on the menu, but he kept wondering if Monique Martel was actually going to show up.

He had just settled on something to order for himself when a petite blond appeared in front of him, wearing a dark-cherry sheath dress and matching beret.

"Sorry I'm late, but traffic was heavy. You are Mark, right?"

He stood and somehow managed to speak with a steady voice. "Yes, I am." He pulled out the chair opposite his, then immediately wondered if men were still allowed to perform this courtesy. "Your outfit looks terrific." Was that too trite? Maybe Monique wouldn't like his majoring on her physical appearance. She might be one of those women who wanted to be respected for her brain.

Monique smiled charmingly. Apparently he'd done okay so far.

He briefly wondered if her hair was naturally blond, then chastised himself for even thinking about that.

Between comments on the restaurant, the weather, and the menu, conversation flowed easily. When the waitress asked for their drink orders, Monique seemed surprised by his choice of ginger ale. But his brief explanation about an alcoholic father seemed to clear that up.

After the server delivered a lamb curry dish for her and roast pork for him, Monique glanced at him with a smile. "I'd love to hear about your work at the US consulate. What is it you really do?"

Between bites, he tried to explain his duties: granting visas to non-US citizens wanting to travel in the States, visiting Americans in jail or seriously ill patients in the hospital, interviewing young people applying to study in American universities.

"I'm confused." Her Quebecois accent attracted him. "Aren't you a CIA agent?" She leaned closer and whispered, "A spy?"

What has his friend told her about him? "A spy? In Canada?"

She shrugged.

"Have you ever heard of the Five Eyes countries?"

She shook her head. "Sounds like a cheesy horror movie."

He took in a deep breath. "Canada, Britain, Australia, New Zealand, and the United States share intelligence. We're democracies."

She pouted prettily. "What about France?"

Mark had heard something commendable about France lately. Ah, yes. At the conference he recently attended. "At an economic summit in Toronto earlier this summer, Canada, France, the US, Germany, Japan, the UK, and Italy all agreed to work together on economic reforms."

"Oh."

He scrambled for a topic Monique might be more interested in. "Have you seen any good movies lately?"

Her eyes brightened. "Yes!"

His moviegoing experiences for the past few years had mostly been ones he could enjoy with his children. But Monique had apparently seen every movie shown in Montreal since her babyhood. And she delighted in reviewing them for Mark's pleasure.

As they were finishing dessert, the pager in his pocket beeped. Being the consulate duty officer for the week, he'd had to keep it with him.

"Sorry." He pulled it out. "I've got to find a pay phone. Be back in a minute." He grabbed his briefcase from under the table.

Monique gaped at him as if his spy nimbus had advanced to a golden halo.

He found a phone on a nearby corner, dropped in the correct change, and called the number on his pager. With a sinking feeling, he recognized it as belonging to his law-enforcement friend Olivier St. Arnoud, a member of the Sûreté du Québec.

This can't be good.

"Olivier? Mark here."

"Sorry to bother you on the weekend. But we have a little problem."

Mark's mental antennae vibrated. In Olivier's profession, a situation described at first as a "little problem" seldom was—no more than a root canal was a slight dental problem.

"What's up?"

"It seems one of your citizens has been killed in an automobile collision. Name's William Ernest Bancroft."

Mark tightened his hand around the phone receiver. Olivier would not be called to the scene of a mere accident. Nor would he be notifying Mark about it.

"Not an accident, I presume?"

"We believe it was intentional."

"How do you know the nationality?" If the victim wasn't an American, he wouldn't need to be involved.

"We will need more positive identification, but the passport in his glove compartment is a good indication. Could you meet me at the scene?"

Olivier gave directions to an address in a warehouse district close to the river. Mark cradled the receiver and scribbled on the small notepad he always kept in his shirt pocket.

Returning to the restaurant, he considered how to politely disengage from Monique. To his surprise, he felt a bit of relief at the excuse to end their date.

She sat upright as he neared, clearly eager for his explanation.

"I apologize, Monique, but I've got to take care of a . . . little problem."

"What kind of problem?" She practically bounced in her seat.

"Sorry. It's confidential."

Her upraised eyebrows and knowing smile indicated intense interest. Mark grabbed the check and helped Monique scoot back her chair. Good thing they'd come in separate vehicles.

After quickly paying the bill, he walked her to her car, an Audi Quattro. He mumbled another apology and managed to leave before she asked more questions. Like when he would see her again. Without looking back, he headed for his Plymouth Voyager.

So much for his first date since Reye. And his plans for a quiet weekend.

CHAPTER TWO

*M*ark cautiously approached the crash site. The twisted body of the victim lay partially hidden under a canvas tarp a few feet away from the driver's side of a mangled Volkswagen Beetle. The windshield had been broken from the inside, indicating it had probably been rammed from behind. But no second car was parked near it. A hit-and-run?

The driver must not have worn a seat belt. Mark made a mental note to bear down on his children about the importance of seat belts. Did this driver have children at home? Who would Mark need to notify of the death? Wife? Parent? Grown son or daughter?

A policeman held back a small group of watchers. The surrounding midrise buildings, not ancient enough to be turned into apartments, dominated the area.

Olivier St. Arnoud, short and slim with a trim mustache, motioned for the policeman to allow Mark to enter the roped-off area. A French-speaking Quebecois, Olivier greeted Mark in English. "Sorry to interrupt your weekend."

"Yours as well." Mark spoke passable French but only the standard version he'd learned in college.

Standing beside Olivier, he noticed several books littering the ground in front of the car. They must have sprung from the front trunk, spewed out by the impact. He glanced at the victim. "What can you tell me about him?"

Olivier stepped to a small table that held papers and other items. He picked up a small booklet with the image of an eagle on the dark front cover and handed it to Mark.

He opened it to the title page. The headshot was of a dark-haired man with a bushy beard covering half of his face, showing hints of gray. His head seemed large, perhaps influenced by his balding forehead. His lips didn't smile the way most would have for a picture.

"William Ernest Bancroft was born in California on September 7, 1944," he read aloud.

"The passport was issued in San Francisco on July 20, 1984," Olivier said.

Mark stifled a shiver. Bancroft was born on Mark's birthday exactly ten years earlier.

"Another West Coast beginning," he said, referring to the stolen American passport in the case he and St. Arnoud had worked on recently.

Olivier moved toward the body, and Mark hesitantly followed.

Olivier removed the cover. The victim's face was barely recognizable, with numerous jagged gashes. The right side of his head, caved in and bloodied, must have hit the pavement after his trip through the windshield.

Mark wished his supper hadn't been so rich.

Olivier re-covered the body. They stepped carefully to the Volkswagen.

Mark checked the passport for a next of kin. But that section was blank. He wished more Americans understood how important NOK information was should they be hospitalized or die in a foreign country. Perhaps it was human nature to avoid such reminders.

"Any idea where his family is?"

Olivier gestured toward the table. "Records in the glove compartment indicate he is a landed immigrant to Canada through his wife, Clair Nicole Trimblay Bancroft. They married slightly less than four years ago. Might indicate a plan. Perhaps he was leaving some sort of troublesome

10

past. Get your US passport, then move to Canada with your wife and obtain landed immigrant status? The address on the papers is out of date, so we haven't been able to locate the wife yet."

Mark extracted the notepad and ballpoint from his shirt pocket. He scribbled the names and dates from Bancroft's paperwork, then returned the notepad and pen to his pocket. He slid the passport into his briefcase. "The wife does appear to be Canadian."

"Possibly a dual national," Olivier suggested. "Perhaps they met in California."

Mark sighed. "Any witnesses?"

St. Arnoud shook his head. "One man leaving late from work in a nearby building says he heard the crash. By the time he got here, he only saw the smashed vehicle."

Mark frowned. "Hit-and-run then."

Olivier tilted his head. "We have not yet apprehended the other driver. But we believe the accident was planned."

"You think the intention was to kill Bancroft?"

Olivier led the way to the Beetle, avoiding the detached door on the pavement. He pointed to a short section of a seat belt an inch or so from its attachment into the floorboard. The rest of the belt, still fastened together, lay on the passenger seat.

Mark squinted at it. "Not just defective?"

"No. Look here, close to where the belt comes up from the floor of the car. There's a partial slash mark on the remaining bit of the belt. That wasn't torn away. And that's not enough to have come loose with a tug on the strap, as would've happened if Bancroft had pulled it."

"Murder then."

"A strong case for it, at least."

"But why would someone go to all this trouble? Why not just waylay him and shoot him?"

"Possibly because they thought no one would notice a severed seat belt, and the crash would be considered an accident."

Mark followed Olivier to the scattered books ejected from the front trunk of the car. A cardboard box lay nearby—probably what the victim had been carrying them in.

"We haven't closely examined those yet, but the titles indicate our man had a strong interest in politics and economics."

Mark stooped and glanced at the titles of a few: two copies of the classic *Leviathan* by Thomas Hobbes, a tattered hardback by John Stuart Mill, title too faded to read, and several books whose authors he didn't recognize. And the perennial college textbook on economics, *The Worldly Philosophers* by Robert Heilbroner. Mark had studied that one himself in his basic econ course.

He noted one of a darker nature: *Memoirs of a Revolutionist* by Peter Kropotkin, someone vaguely familiar to Mark as a Russian anarchist. Even more disturbing, a book on ecoterrorism. Merely a guide to the subject, or actually espousing it?

A hazy picture formed in Mark's mind. He envisioned the Haight-Ashbury district in San Francisco a couple of decades or so ago, scene of the hippie counterculture. Bancroft would've been in his twenties, perhaps beginning on that beard.

"Do you think he might have been killed by a revolutionary he was involved with? Or knew something about?"

"If he took advantage of his wife's citizenship to move to Canada to escape something, someone might have found out where he was."

"I'll find whatever records we have on him based on the passport data. Run a check on any passport for the wife as well."

Mark sensed in his gut that this was going to be the most challenging task he'd ever faced on his job.

CHAPTER THREE

*M*ark drove through Montreal's main business district to the office building housing the US consulate. He showed his ID to the guard, then took the elevator to the fourth floor. His steps echoed in the weekend quiet. The last rays of sun from side windows outlined empty desks.

His first duty was notifying the State Department, where a crew always worked around the clock. Foreign Service officers referred to it as their 911 call center.

A woman's crisp voice informed him that he'd reached the Operations Center. He notified her that an American had been killed in Montreal in an accident under suspicious circumstances, then provided particulars from the passport. He also told her what he knew about Bancroft's wife and requested a search for any information from their passport applications.

If the wife was confirmed as an American, he would need to call her—or visit her if she lived in the district. Assuming she was still alive.

He phoned his boss, Mike Putnam, consul general for the Montreal consulate. Marcia, his wife, answered and put Mike on the line immediately.

"Hey, Mark. What's happening?"

Mark heard sounds of a social gathering in the background. "Sorry to bother you." He briefly outlined the wreck and Olivier St. Arnoud's suspicions.

"I hope it isn't a case of an American wife murdering her American husband."

That thought had flitted through Mark's mind. "Trying not to jump to conclusions."

"Of course."

After confirming that Mark had notified the Department, Mike hung up to return to his dinner party.

Mark checked his files but found no record of either Bancroft or his wife. Not unexpected, since Bancroft's passport had been issued in San Francisco. He composed a cable to go out on Monday morning when communications opened. Then he returned home, where his family would no doubt beg to know how his date went.

That seemed so long ago he wasn't sure he could remember enough to tell them about it. Maybe the twins would be in bed. But his mother would certainly be waiting, and she'd grill him like he was a teenager.

CHAPTER FOUR

*M*ark pulled into the driveway of the 1920s bungalow he was renting for his family during his Montreal tour. He was grateful for his widowed mother, Deedra Pacer, and his mother-in-law, Melba Quinnell, also widowed, who had helped so much with the twins, Deedee and Sean, after Reye's death. But he did not relish the thought of his family's interrogation about his date.

His mother had seemed delighted that Mark was finally going out. Deedee had wanted him to find out if his date liked children. "You won't marry somebody like Cruella de Vil, will you?" They had recently watched a TV rerun of the Disney movie featuring the dark villainess who liked to kill Dalmatians to make a coat from their skins.

Did she harbor a fear that a stepmother might threaten her status? His daughter thrived in imaginative realms, already scribbling short stories of children having adventures and solving mysteries.

"If I begin dating somebody on a regular basis, I'll be sure to include the family," Mark promised. "You can judge her for yourselves."

"Are you going to kiss her, Dad?" Sean had asked.

Mark dreaded the idea of having to report to his family every moment of his relationship with a female. "I don't know," he said. "But that kind of thing is private."

Sean had not seemed satisfied with that answer.

What would his own reactions be when Sean and Deedee began dating?

He and Reye were both brought up by parents who were active in small-town churches. They had followed the ways they'd been taught and shown. "Coupling" was reserved for after the wedding vows, and they had acquiesced to the rule.

In this latest of his Foreign Service postings, the children were attending a Catholic school, though Mark was Protestant. Of the choices offered, that one seemed closest to the working-class ethos in which he was raised.

The career he had chosen might send him, at some point in the future, to a post where the only communal school choice was an upper-class private school. Mark wasn't sure how he would handle that. Maybe have one of the grandmothers teach them at home?

He rolled the word *home* around in his mind. How long had it been since he'd gone back to that small Appalachian town he grew up in? Did it still exist in any way as he remembered it?

His mother returned occasionally to visit family and friends, but he had not gone to Mocking Bird for several years. Letters between Mark and Jeremy, his best friend growing up, had lessened to brief messages scrawled on Christmas cards. Even those had disappeared when Mark stopped sending them following Reye's death.

After parking the Voyager in the garage, he sat for a moment as a sense of uneasiness nibbled at his peace of mind. Cables and articles he'd read at work about the nuclear weapons the United States and the Soviet Union still held made him nervous about the future his kids would face. Not to mention the small groups coming together in various places, fomenting hatred inspired by centuries-old ethnic conflicts. And those wanting to destroy any form of government.

And what about Egypt's attack on the US embassy last year? No one could neatly label events by Cold War antagonists anymore. Who were these people?

More relevant to his personal life, who was William Bancroft? And why had he been studying those books that had spilled from the trunk of his Volkswagen?

Mark shook off the shadowy thoughts and got out of the car. He wished Reye were here to rescue him from his dark musings.

• • • • •

When Mark entered the living room, his mom turned off the television, rose to greet him, then settled back in her recliner while Mark sat on the couch.

"How was your evening?" she asked casually, though he knew she was dying to hear details of what was surely a major interest after Mark's apparently long evening with Monique.

"It got steamrolled by a duty officer call. I had to leave early and go to the scene of a traffic accident. An American citizen was killed."

Having lived in Mark's household since she and the twins joined him in Egypt, she knew him well enough to realize that something besides a simple accident was involved. "Were others injured?"

"No."

Unlike Monique Martel, Deedra Pacer was not overwhelmed by any glamour associated with Mark's job. "Did your call interrupt a budding relationship?"

"To be honest, it was somewhat of a relief. Monique had the impression I'm a spy for the CIA. I'm sure I would've been a disappointment to her."

"Oh, that's too bad." She sighed.

His mother had seemed a bit tired lately. Was taking care of the kids too much for her? He owed a priceless debt for the love and attention she provided them, allowing him to concentrate on his job without worrying about babysitters.

Did she need a rest from the constant duty? Maybe she wanted more time to visit relatives and old friends—although, to all outward observation, she had reveled in her experiences in the countries where Mark was stationed.

She stared at the blank TV screen. "Are you still on for the hike tomorrow? The twins are really looking forward to it."

Mark yawned, fatigue finally overcoming the adrenaline. "I'll have to check in with the ops center before we go, find out if somebody uncovered anything on our accident victim."

She nodded, sighed, then slowly pushed herself out of the recliner. After wishing him a good night, she left for her bedroom.

Mark lay awake for hours thinking about William Ernest Bancroft. On a Washington assignment a few years ago, he'd worked a case that originated with someone previously involved in the Northern California hippie scene. What was the name?

Just as he was drifting off to sleep, it flashed into his mind.

Rooney Steiger.

CHAPTER FIVE

With his duty officer beeper and phone numbers stowed in his hiking backpack, Mark reminded Deedra, "If I get a work call, tell them to beep me." As he shepherded the twins out the door, he wondered if there were pay phones on the mountain.

He should have planned the hike when he wasn't the consulate's duty officer for the week.

Weekend traffic was heavy, with everyone enjoying late-summer activities. But Mark found a parking spot close to the walk leading up Mount Royal, the summit for which Montreal was named.

The twins raced ahead of Mark like projectiles propelled by a cannon.

Sean glanced back a time or two to make sure his father was following. Probably still a bit haunted by that accidental separation from him on the train last spring.

They passed other families, mostly French speakers. And most of the other children were accompanied by a man and a woman.

Why did he feel like an oddity? Plenty of children lived with only one parent—though usually due to divorce these days rather than death.

Of course, some of the pairs might be single parents with significant others.

The last time he had felt so alone was in a northern Virginia hotel room before his orientation for the Foreign Service.

As he trudged around other hikers who appeared satisfied with what life had dealt them, he fought a feeling of homesickness. He wanted old friends and corn bread and fried catfish and people who said "y'all."

The twins sprinted ahead, full of life and energy. But they would grow up, all too soon. What would his life be like then?

When they reached the top of the mountain, he gazed around from the overlook, his loneliness allayed by the view of Montreal's skyline and the St. Lawrence River and the surrounding countryside.

What a gem this city was. Surely one of the more civilized tours for a Foreign Service officer. No worries about dysentery from the water supply, no heavy-handed police force, no stinking jails where a consular officer visited frightened US citizens arrested on frivolous charges.

"Daddy," Deedee said, "could we be Canadians if we wanted to?"

"Well, it would be pretty difficult now, since we're assigned here as a diplomatic family. After you grow up, you could apply for permanent residence here, what they call landed immigrant status. Then, if you were accepted, after a certain number of years living here, you could apply for citizenship."

Actually, he wasn't that familiar with rules for Canadian citizenship. He was tied to the rules for American citizens living abroad, in Canada or elsewhere. He'd never thought about any of his family members desiring any other nationality.

Of course, one of them could marry a Canadian for citizenship—like William Bancroft apparently did.

"I like Canada," Deedee said. "Maybe I'll be Canadian when I grow up."

Sean rolled his eyes. "It is a pretty nice country. But I like Missouri too. Maybe I could be both Canadian and American."

A few people had the good fortune to be citizens of both countries. Olivier St. Arnoud had wondered if Bancroft's wife had been a dual national.

20

He had a bit of double allegiance himself because of his familiarity with Missouri after growing up in Georgia.

How long had it been since he and the twins visited his home state? His mother returned from time to time, but he and the twins usually stayed with their Grandmother Melba in Missouri when they spent furloughs in the States. She had a house big enough for all of them.

Several years ago, his mother had sold her modest home in Mocking Bird to a cousin, then joined Mark's household.

As his children grew, would they drift away from a connection to their father's ancestry?

They returned home that evening tired but comfortable in the happy-go-lucky state of relaxed exhaustion that follows exertion. As the sun began to set, they prepared for their traditional Sabbath rest.

After supper Mark sprawled on the couch and read Pat Conroy's *The Great Santini* while the children played Parcheesi. Deedra read *The Globe and Mail* in her recliner.

He laid the book on his chest. "I'd like to take a trip back to Mocking Bird during my next leave."

Her focus remained on her newspaper. "Just you?"

"All of us, including the twins."

The twins looked up from their game.

Deedra's eyes brightened. "I'm sure the family would love to see you. They'd especially like to spend time with the children. You haven't been back since Deedee and Sean were quite small."

Sean rolled the dice onto the game board, but his sister stared vacantly, indicating her thoughts were somewhere else.

Mark's mind returned to the name of the man he'd remembered last night. Rooney Steiger was a friend of a friend. During Mark's tour at the State Department, a fellow watch officer had gotten in trouble for sharing confidential information with his friend Steiger. Rooney was a member of a fringe group in the sixties that went beyond civil disobedience to skirting anarchy. He had even been suspected of attempting to blow up a dam in California.

Could Bancroft have had connections with a group like Steiger's?

Probably not close ones, as he had been cleared for Canadian landed immigrant status.

On Monday he'd touch base with Olivier St. Arnoud and check for any information about Bancroft that could be gleaned from his US passport application.

• • • • •

As they exited the sanctuary on Sunday, Mark waved to John Morris, one of the ministers of the Anglican church they attended, who was surrounded by members of the congregation. He and John hadn't talked in a while. Mark considered setting a time to meet with him over lunch someday.

That afternoon, following dinner and a game of Scrabble with the twins, Mark pulled out an old set of encyclopedias his father had bought with precious money years ago. Drayton Pacer had read them like a best-selling novel. Almost every Sunday afternoon, he sat in his easy chair, feet relaxed on the hassock, and devoured various topics, then discussed with his family some fact that had fascinated him.

Mark kept the set more for sentimental reasons than anything else, but he pulled out the A volume and thumbed until he found *anarchism.*

In college history courses, the concept had surfaced in the history of certain countries—France during the French Revolution and the formation of the Soviet Union, for example.

He read several entries on the subject and discovered that *anarchy* meant "without authority." Yet some groups who rejected one aspect of that authority, like the ones dealing with state religious mandates, could be peaceful.

Religious groups like Anabaptists wanted to withdraw from society and live harmoniously within their group. Coming into existence when the great nationalist/religious wars began during the sixteenth century, they were Christian pacifists. Most of them were persecuted out of existence, but one group survived under a leader named Menno Simons. They became known as the Mennonites, with some members settling in North America.

Other groups, though not religious, also did not advocate the violent overthrow of government. They thought of government, particularly the ownership of property, as a restraint that needed to be loosened. For some, this meant the rejection of any rules for the protection of private property.

Other groups rejected authority in their search for a higher state, seeking a retreat from the material world. Many of them desired a society based on cooperation, not coercion by government.

Mark perused a section about Pierre-Joseph Proudhon, a French writer and socialist who moved more toward the "order of anarchy" and the rejection of political authority. In that day, some rulers reigned as monarchs with absolute power. Easy to understand why some might wish to abolish authority, violently if necessary.

But in the United States?

He returned to his reading. Karl Marx, Peter Kropotkin, and others added their ideas. The means of production should be owned by all. Distribution should be shared collectively. You don't gain freedom through laws and parliaments, some said, but through a proletariat of the people. The idea evolved, but not into peaceful communities of sharers. Instead, some advocated workers forcibly overthrowing governments.

The first nation to be overtaken forcibly by communism was a less industrialized nation, Russia. That example not only led to a bloody aftermath but demonstrated how quickly the ideal of no government could degenerate into rule by a privileged few.

Meanwhile, the United States, a capitalist nation, survived the Great Depression and became a superpower, a leader in the defeat of the Nazis. That same nation led in maintaining a certain level of peace through the years of the Cold War, at least as far as major wars were concerned.

The encyclopedia was published in 1960, the year Mark entered first grade. Current anarchist movements weren't covered. His adolescence in the late 1960s was spent in a conservative Appalachian community. The momentous events of that decade were distant noises echoing events far away.

Years later, because of a friend's involvement with Rooney Steiger, Mark had briefly researched his group, operating in Northern California. Mark's friend on the State Department's watch, in a youthful rebellion against a wealthy but unfeeling father, had flirted in his college years with Steiger's group, though he had never been an anarchist. Such involvement would have barred him from a career in the Foreign Service.

Today, with the anarchism that spawned the Soviet Union and a world communist movement now seemingly tamed, anarchist ideas had entered a new phase. As before, some were peaceful, advocating simple movements toward withdrawal into nature. Others seemed bent on tearing down a society they considered corrupt and beyond redemption.

Mark's friend departed from Steiger's influence when he decided to become a diplomat. But Steiger had shown up in the friend's life one day, and the friend had allowed himself to be compromised.

Anarchism had influenced Steiger and other young Americans. Movements sprang up against capitalism, including a few acts of terrorism. The circled "A" made its appearance as a symbol of the anarchist movement.

What had happened to Rooney Steiger and his friends since then? Surely, within the small groups operating in Haight-Ashbury and in communes around Northern California, Steiger and the recently murdered Bancroft had at least known of each other.

Mark returned his attention to the encyclopedia volume.

So-called true believers often fell out with each other over leadership, even starting bloody feuds. Leon Trotsky had worked with Vladimir Lenin in creating the Soviet Union during World War I. After Lenin's death, Trotsky lost out to Josef Stalin as the next head of that country. Eventually, Trotsky fled to Mexico. That did not save him from Stalin's wrath. As World War II was beginning, he was murdered by a Stalinist agent.

Idealists, it seemed, were as subject to the deadly temptations of power as anyone else.

CHAPTER SIX

ark left a still sleeping household earlier than usual after a quick breakfast of oatmeal, canned peaches, and coffee. He reached the consulate offices before they came alive for the day. He spoke for a few minutes with Joyce Minnick, the new junior consular officer.

Joyce, single, in her mid-twenties, was a second tour junior officer, "coned," as the vocational slot was called for Foreign Service officers in the consular branch. All officers usually spent one of their first tours "out of cone." She had spent her previous tour in an administrative position in Mumbai, India. Of average looks, with medium-length, slightly curly brown hair, she possessed the most important trait of a good consular officer: the ability to listen. She often went out socially with the younger Canadian staffers.

After settling in his office, Mark called the State Department operations center to follow up on his Friday evening call. The consular duty officer had pulled information from the passport application of William Ernest Bancroft, verifying the information Olivier had given Mark.

Other information listed Bancroft's California address in Oakland. The officer had contacted the current occupants of that address. They had lived there going on two years and had no knowledge of any previous occupants.

Bancroft had listed his mother for the parent section of the application, no father.

Ruby Anne Bancroft, a US citizen, was born in Lawton, Oklahoma, in 1927. Had Bancroft's parents, or perhaps only his mother, left Oklahoma in the grand migration of Okies and Arkies to the California promised land? Some left during the Depression, others during the war years when West Coast jobs were booming. A few of Mark's Appalachian relatives had done the same, their names now vanished from the memory of all but the oldest of his kin.

Ruby Anne Bancroft would have been seventeen years old when her son was born, in a state far removed from that of her family and friends.

The State Department officer also had gathered information on Bancroft's wife. Clair Nicole Trimblay Bancroft was born in Redding, California, on June 2, 1950. She had applied for a US passport on the same day as her husband in San Francisco. Like Bancroft, she was a Californian, but her family name indicated Quebecois origins. Her father was born in 1920 in Trois-Rivières, Quebec, Canada. He was living at the time of the application and was a US citizen. Apparently Clair Bancroft and her parents were dual nationals of the US and Canada.

Neither William Bancroft nor his wife listed any previous passports.

Mark had barely hung up from that call when his phone rang.

"We've found the wife," Olivier said. "We notified her of her husband's death. She was stoic. As though she was expecting it."

Interesting reaction.

"She said they were not living together. In fact, they were considering a legal separation, but not immediately. They agreed to wait so his status as a landed immigrant would not be endangered. She has degrees in childhood education and earns money as a freelance editor of school textbooks. Her husband lived in a small apartment behind the used bookstore he operated, which explains all those books he was carrying around. She said he often bought old books at garage sales and estate closings."

Mark sat up straighter. "Isn't the partner almost always a suspect when there are problems in a marriage and one of them is murdered?"

"Killed," Olivier corrected. "Since it's all still under investigation, we did not tell her of our suspicions. Only that it is at present being treated as a hit-and-run."

"Can you give me her address?"

"Of course. She lives in St. Henri, as did her husband." Olivier supplied the address. "She is a dual national. Born in 1950 in California to Canadian citizens through whom she obtained her Canadian citizenship. They emigrated to California just before the Second World War, and her father took a job as an accountant. Both parents still living there now. Also a brother."

"Children?"

"No. But I sensed she was holding something back. I wonder if she and Bancroft were into some activity not quite legitimate. Anti-government, perhaps? Maybe related to those student protests in California universities. Then perhaps there was a falling out. Did they anger someone? Both were well educated and surely could find good jobs there, but there is no evidence that they came to Canada for employment reasons."

"They might have been escaping something. Somebody with a grudge perhaps."

"I told her you might be contacting her because of her and her husband's US nationality."

"I'll call her as soon as I can."

"I am concerned, Mark. You weren't here during the troubles in the '60s. The books Bancroft was carrying around . . . anarchy is something I do not want to see here."

"Of course not."

"Perhaps Bancroft's job as a bookseller was more of a hobby to feed his own perceived occupation as a philosopher. Something to pay the bills while he philosophized. The question is whether it may have been a front for more serious activities."

"I'll see what I can find out." Mark shuddered at the thought of what he might find out.

CHAPTER SEVEN

*M*ark studied the brick apartment complex, converted from a former industrial warehouse, where Clair Nicole Trimblay Bancroft lived. The apartments in the four-story edifice were lower-grade fashionable, within walking distance of neighborhood shopping and the metro. The kind favored by young seekers of the urban lifestyle.

Still, the apartments wouldn't be cheap. Surely Bancroft's income from his used bookstore wouldn't enable him to help his wife much with the rent. Maybe her book editing gave her whatever else they needed. Did she also have money from her parents?

He had called her, expressed condolences, and asked if he could visit with her.

She responded that she very much wanted to meet with him and talk about her husband, but her voice seemed hesitant. That was to be expected; after all, she was still adjusting to her loss, even if she hadn't been on the best of terms with her husband.

He entered the building and climbed the stairway to her apartment on the second floor.

"Hello, Mr. Pacer. Please come in." She stepped aside for him to enter.

Her accent was California American but held a softness that might have been a Quebecois remnant lingering from her parents, no doubt increased by return to her parents' country of birth.

She was slender and slightly below Mark's height. Mid-length cinnamon-brown hair, neatly trimmed with an outwardly curled flip at the end. Her eyes, slightly darker than her hair, looked at him without embarrassment, as though ready to take on anything life threw at her.

"I'm so sorry about your husband, Ms. Bancroft. Thank you for agreeing to see me."

She gestured him into a small sitting area with a couple of canvas chairs and a small couch. Books lined one wall on plank-and-brick bookcases. Mark scanned the neatly arranged books. The titles did not suggest subjects as heavy as her husband's tastes appeared to be.

Lots of children's books. An old one he remembered from his childhood, something about a boy and his horse. A few were college textbooks on education. Mystery collections filled most of two shelves—Dorothy Sayers, Tony Hillerman, P. D. James.

She adjusted the curtains, opened the window, then waved him to the small couch. She sat in one of the canvas chairs, legs uncrossed, back straight, hands folded in her lap. He was reminded of one of his early elementary school teachers, the one he and the other young boys fell in love with.

"Ms. Bancroft, I'll be happy to help you with whatever papers you might need for doing business in the States. We're required to write an official report of death, for example. You may wish to have a copy."

"Thank you." Her strong features changed to those of a supplicant. "Mr. Pacer, were you at the location of the accident?"

"Yes. An hour or two after it happened."

"Do you think he suffered a great deal?"

"It appeared that he died as soon as he was ejected from the car." He hoped that matched what the Canadians had told her.

"He always wore a seat belt. They said it broke. I find that strange."

"Yes, ma'am. I believe the authorities are looking into that." He decided on as much openness as possible. "Do you have any reason to think the collision might have been intentional?"

"Yes, I do. I know of people who would want him dead."

He startled at her immediate transparency.

"Back in California, Bill and I belonged to a peace group. Some people called them hippies. After the Vietnam War ended, groups began mobilizing around issues like getting back to nature, living off the land, without a formal government."

"I've heard about them." Mark tried not to sound judgmental, in spite of what people in his neck of the woods had thought about "those long-haired hippie types."

She focused on her hands, folded in her lap. "It was such a vibrant time. We were concerned about the terrible cost of war and about how governments abetted those wars. We were young and thought we had the answers to everything."

The distant look in her eyes told him she saw something beyond this small apartment and the dust motes dancing in the sunlight streaming through the window.

"Your accent is lovely." Her face registered an open curiosity. "You are from the South, aren't you? Southern United States, I mean."

"Mocking Bird, Georgia." He needed to bring the conversation back to the matter at hand. "You and your husband met through your interests in political involvement?"

Clair nodded. "Bill attended the University of California, Berkeley, majoring in philosophy, going for his master's. I was studying education at Pacific Oaks in San Jose. We met through mutual acquaintances and were just friends when we became members of a peace group. Bill was deeply into a study of schools of thought emphasizing nonviolence."

Mark tried to imagine the philosophy department in a liberal Northern California university in the 1960s and '70s, about as far away from his teenage years as possible.

"When the Vietnam War intensified, we couldn't understand why the United States was involved in a local war so far away. Bill and I become involved in more serious protest movements after the Kent State killings."

"Yes, I read about that." He had been in high school when it happened, more concerned about trying to find a way to afford college.

"After I graduated in 1972," Clair continued, "I entered graduate school in education. We became concerned about nuclear war, too, appalled at the possibility that nuclear weapons could actually be used to destroy civilization. Bill and I intended to protest only nonviolently, though."

Their types had been called "peaceniks," Mark remembered. "Did you participate in the march on Washington?"

"That was before I started college, but Bill was involved. After I got to know him, it seemed natural for me to become a part of the peace movement too. We got to know some people we trusted at first, then found out they wanted to go too far. When we decided to opt out of the less peaceful activities, we were told we couldn't because Bill owed them money. Berkley's an expensive school. Bill had a scholarship for his graduate program, but it covered only tuition."

"Was his family originally from California?"

"No." She looked up from her hands and faced him. "Bill never knew his father. His mother left Oklahoma during World War II when she was pregnant with Bill. Bill's father was drafted soon after he was conceived and apparently never knew he had a son. His mother never even told Bill his name."

Mark thought of how different her life might have been as an unwed mother in a small rural community.

Clair smiled. "My family took advantage of the boom in jobs but in more fortunate circumstances than Bill's. My father was an accountant from Trois-Rivières—just down the St. Lawrence from here. When he got a job offer for a better position in California, he took it. My brother and I were born there."

"What happened to Bill's mother?"

"She died before I met him. He had overcome a lot of obstacles, and he always cheered for the less well-off. He became close to my family, especially my father and brother, even though I know they worried about the activities Bill and I chose to be involved in."

Mark remained silent, not wanting to break her train of thought.

"The leader of the group we had joined, a man named Rooney, attacked a professor, a bystander at one of our demonstrations. Fortunately, he wasn't seriously injured, but it sparked a certain vengefulness in Rooney we hadn't been aware of. He didn't want peace. He wanted a war of his own, which he would control."

Mark had managed not to visibly startle at the name Rooney.

"Bill and I wanted peaceful changes. We favored George McGovern for president. We joined the group because we thought they believed in peaceful change too."

"But it didn't?"

"People are tested when they gain a little power, even over a small group. Bill finally had to admit that Rooney had become more warlike than the people in Washington we were trying to change."

"But the leader, Rooney, made it difficult for you to break away?"

"That's right. We finally decided to move to Canada, like other antiwar protestors had done. For us, it was relatively easy because of my Canadian citizenship."

Mark wanted to find out more about their breaking away from Rooney Steiger. "Do you feel yourself in danger now?"

"Maybe."

Mark could tell she was frightened. He hoped she would share more if he allowed her time.

"That's one reason Bill and I haven't been living together. He was easygoing, while I'm more of a hard charger. Maybe we would have divorced eventually, or maybe we would have gotten back together. But I decided it was safer for me if we didn't live together. We didn't even meet. But we spoke by phone almost every day."

"Do the Canadians know of your apprehension?"

"Yes. They told me to call them if I saw any evidence of being followed or harassed."

"Is your family aware of what's happening?"

"I've told them. I asked them not to visit me yet. They were concerned at that."

"Do you feel it's not safe for them here?"

"I don't want the people who murdered Bill to make any connections with my family."

She seemed certain her husband's death was not an accident.

"I'm not sure they're interested in me, though. Bill's the one who wrote tracts for them and was involved in the planning meetings. He tried so hard to tone down Rooney's anger."

"How?"

"Just a peaceful, behind-the-scenes push for the things he wanted, carrying on conversations with people who came into his bookstore. He hoped our children could grow up in a better world." She glanced away.

Mark felt a need to lessen the tension. "I can identify. I have two children of my own."

She seemed relieved. "What ages?"

"Both are seven. Twins. A boy and a girl. Their mother died a few years ago."

Her face blanched. "I'm so sorry."

"Thank you. My mother lives with us, and she is a godsend." Why had he brought his private life into this conversation?

He shifted forward, indicating his intention to leave. "I appreciate your seeing me today. I'll be in touch. When we have all the information from the Canadian authorities, could I meet with you again—here or at the consulate?"

"Of course."

"If there's anything you need, give me a call." He handed her his card, on which he had scribbled his home number next to the business one.

They rose, and she followed him to the door.

Back in his car, as he pulled out of his parking space, he almost veered into the path of an oncoming car, jerking to a halt just in time to avoid a collision. The other driver gestured at him, then continued on.

Had Rooney Steiger threatened Bill and Clair if they didn't perform some illegal activity? Her description of Steiger invited all sorts of historic comparisons. Hitler, Stalin, and others with persuasive control: an illusion of profound purpose hiding an evil lust for power.

CHAPTER EIGHT

Restless and unable to find resolution for his unsettling new feelings, Mark considered asking out Monique Martel again. Twice he picked up the phone in his office to do so, and each time returned it without dialing.

No, he didn't want more time with Monique. He wanted time with Clair Bancroft. He felt more of a connection with her, perhaps just because they were both widowed.

But her loss was too recent. She needed time to adjust to the violent death of her husband. Mark should at least wait a decent interval before— what exactly, he didn't know.

When she came to the consulate for her husband's report of death, that might be the last time he would see her. Why would she stay in Canada? Her academic training had prepared her to teach, but she appeared to have made no movements in that direction here. She seemed to have no close relations with any of her relatives or friends in Canada. Her only family was in California. She had grown up there and no doubt had friends as well.

The report of William Ernest Bancroft's death came through in about a week. Cause of death: concussion to the head due to an automobile accident. Nothing about possible criminal action.

He did not contact Clair right away. Instead, he called John Morris, the pastor of the church he and his family attended. He arranged to meet him for lunch in a sandwich shop at noon the next day.

• • • • •

When Mark arrived at the small restaurant, he found John, dressed in casual layman's attire, sitting at a yellow laminate table against a side wall. Lost in a book, he looked up quickly when Mark pulled out the opposite chair.

"Must be interesting," Mark said.

John pushed the book aside. "I just bought this. It's a history of the Jesus Movement in the '70s."

The waitress arrived, and they gave her their orders: a fish sandwich for John, a BLT for Mark.

"I remember that," Mark said. "I entered college at the tail end of it. It was a Christian university, so Jesus was well known there even without the Jesus Movement."

The waitress set glasses of water on the table, then left.

"Americans fled to Canada to avoid the draft during that era. Many of them have strong opinions about what they've done, one way or another. But I was pretty much untouched by it all. How about you?" He figured John to be about a decade older than him.

John smiled. "You are looking at a faded flower child. Drugs, free love, and all that."

"Really?"

The waitress delivered their food. Between bites, John told his story.

"My father fought for Britain and the empire during World War II. Served in Asia, but managed to come through without serious injury. Glad to come home to peace and prosperity in North America."

"Tell me about your family."

"I have one sister, five years older than I am. My family attended church at Easter, but that was about it. My sister got pregnant and married the father. I lived with them and my nephew Brian my first year in university, along with my girlfriend, Chelsea. They're the ones who started me on drugs."

"We fought this big war for democracy and freedom," Mark mused, "and then didn't know what to do with the new prosperity."

"Oh, we knew what to do with it. Make love, not war. Have drug-ins and love-ins."

Mark shook his head. "But there was a serious element to it, right? A sobering realization that we could destroy the planet?"

"There was a Christian peace movement. And part of it was this Jesus people thing. Alan, my brother-in-law, found it after he almost died of a drug overdose."

Mark had wondered about John's story, something he had never talked about. "A wake-up experience for your brother-in-law?"

John nodded. "Sobered us all. Except for Chelsea, who thought we were nuts when we started going to these praise gatherings in the basement of an old church. Some elderly women welcomed in people like us for food and Jesus. Something happened inside me there. Eventually I had to choose between Chelsea and Jesus. Long story short, Chelsea left. I got Jesus. Never regretted the exchange."

"But you're still not married."

He looked off into space. "Someday, maybe. I still have too much growing up to do. So much to learn."

Mark turned his thoughts to what he had wanted to share when he set up this meeting. "In your connections with various movements during that time, did you ever encounter any anarchists?"

John grinned. "Oh, yes. Most were peaceful, back-to-nature types."

The waitress brought their checks.

"It's a beautiful day," John said. "What do you say we find a park bench and talk some more?"

They found one close to McGill University. After they were settled, Mark said, "There's a wide range of beliefs among anarchist groups, right? Those who simply want to withdraw and those who want to destroy governments."

"That's where I draw the line with anarchists—the militant types. Those who would destroy the state assume we have the power to build a perfect one. I don't believe any of us are capable of that. I ended my youthful rebellion by joining the church, a place for imperfect, fallen humans."

What kind of group had Bill Bancroft belonged to? "You're saying that forming political groups is fine, but actively seeking to tear down society isn't?"

"You've hit it right. My involvement in the peace movement was a peripheral thing. I was just caught up in youthful rebellion."

"But you found your way back to traditional Christian ways?"

"Some serve by withdrawing, others by seeking a more active role. But I'm dead set against tearing down just for the sake of destruction."

"How powerful are the groups today that propose to rebel against the state in order to bring about their idea of an ideal society?"

John studied the sidewalk. "When times are bad—economically or spiritually—the temptation is always to lay waste, not take the slower but infinitely better way of peaceful change. Social action groups? Peacefully waving signs? Sure. Riots, no."

"Which brings us back to the anarchists."

John nodded. "Europe developed central governments much later than places like China and India. But like almost everywhere, a few strong groups tended to take control. Part of my growing religious understanding concluded that the religion of Jesus, when actually practiced, raises up small groups here and there who attempt to live differently. Some set up religious communities."

"Like monasteries and nunneries?"

"Yes, but in a few instances, communities of families."

Mark searched through ideas from his reading. "Cathars? Lollards? Ah, yes, Menno Simons and the Mennonites. Pacifist groups, often persecuted."

"Yes. As the European states developed, they constantly fought each other for power. How would you like it if you were a ruler and wanted to expand your kingdom, but this small group kept telling you fighting was wrong?"

Mark nodded. "As I recall, most of the dissenters were wiped out by torture and execution. Mennonites survived in North America. But members of the Bruderhof were executed in Nazi Germany, though some survived through migration."

"Those aren't the movements you're interested in, though. You asked about radical groups who want regime change, even if it means killing people who disagree with them."

"Yes. It baffles me that someone might wish to bring peace using warlike methods."

"Two awful wars were begun by allegedly Christian nations."

Mark scoffed. "Nations aren't Christian. Only people are."

John recoiled in mock horror. "Oh, my. What apostasy."

Mark laughed.

John returned to the topic. "The activities of the secret police in countries run by supposedly Christian monarchs like the Russian czars led to a host of movements tinged both by atheism and pacifism. And your country's involvement in Vietnam and other places encouraged their growth in North America."

"And continues to this day, even though relations between the United States and the Soviet Union are thawing."

"Sometimes a movement develops its own power. And remember, the anti-war movement included what I'd call fellow travelers. Anti-capitalists, for example. I expect that if Western ideas overcome Soviet ones, capitalism may become something of a religion."

"When does a movement for peace become a movement against a nation-state because it wages war? And is what such groups propose to put in its place any better?"

After a quiet moment, John responded. "That depends on how imperfect a particular nation-state is. Nazi Germany killing people because they weren't Aryans? I would have supported my father's military efforts in World War II."

"How about the American Civil War? I had ancestors on both sides in that one, slave owners and abolitionists."

"Not meaning to be one of those superior Canadians, but if you hadn't fought the British and established your half-free, half-slave nation in the eighteenth century, you'd have remained in the British empire and done away with slavery in 1833 when the empire did."

"I wonder what might have happened if we hadn't been such hotheads in the period leading up to the American Revolution. Maybe if we had bided our time and worked with those in the British government who were favorable to some of our ideas, eventually things might have gotten sorted out without war."

John flashed a "gotcha" grin. "Maybe you'd have ended up like peaceable Canadians. But that only strengthens the argument for the pacifists."

"Except for gross violation of human rights like with the Nazis."

"Granted."

"Plus, you Canadians aren't blameless concerning the rights of the original North Americans."

"I yield to you on that one. But I have known some folks who seemed determined to bring about peace by warlike methods against the state."

"Forcing peace by war?"

"I know people who would kill for the sake of peace."

"You had separatist problems here in the '60s."

"I grew up in Vancouver. I was into my flower-child phase during the separatist movement. But this present group is part of a worldwide movement. I don't know of specific instances of anarchism here. Of course, I can't give you names."

"I understand. But should I be concerned about a connection between such groups in both countries?"

"I think so."

This "not just a car accident" was getting bigger and more complex every hour.

CHAPTER NINE

*M*ark met Clair at the elevator for consulate employees and their visitors. She arrived precisely at the time they had arranged. She wore a mid-length skirt in an earth-green pattern, a white peasant blouse under a light-gray sweater, and flat-heeled shoes. Her tastes ran to what Mark thought of as hippie styles, but on her they seemed an expression of authentic simplicity—not a costume but a way of life, down-to-earth, with an emphasis on fundamentals.

He led her into his office, gesturing to a seat.

She laid a folder on the small table and glanced around before sitting. "It seems so casual here."

He sat opposite her. "You mean with an honor guard and a moat?"

She smiled. "It seems like any other office in Montreal."

"Canada and the United States have the longest unguarded border in the world. The Canadian prime minister is usually the first foreign head of state to visit a new US president. Canadians, particularly Quebecois, would very much like certain differences acknowledged, which we Americans don't always appreciate. However, we do get along pretty well, and we have a huge trading relationship. But you didn't come here to talk about that. How are you, Ms. Bancroft?"

Her smile brightened her face. "Please call me Clair. Thank you for your concern. Bill and I had our differences, but I miss him tremendously.

My parents came up, and we've made arrangements for Bill's body to be shipped back to California. We'll have a family service there."

"They're staying for a while then?"

"They're helping me with matters like insurance and bank accounts. And spending some time with old friends in Trois-Rivières. We've had property there for years, and they've decided it's time to sell it."

"Have you thought about your own next steps?"

"I'm thinking about accomplishing something I planned to do a long time ago—before we moved to Canada. Teaching disadvantaged children."

"Highly commendable."

She leaned closer. "If I may be so bold, Mr. Pacer, how did you manage your life again after you lost your wife?"

"Call me Mark, please." He struggled to answer her question, though he couldn't figure out why. "She died from a heart problem. We weren't expecting it." He thought of speaking about his time in Egypt and how Reye, his best friend as well as his wife, was separated from him by her job. But he knew if he did, he would be fighting tears.

Thankfully, she gave him a reprieve. "I know death isn't something I'll get over quickly and just go about my business."

"No, it's not."

"I have important decisions to make. My parents want me to give up my condo when the lease is up next summer and go live with them. There are good reasons for that." She did not elaborate. "But breaking the connection with Montreal and the life Bill and I had here is hard, even if it was rocky toward the end. I've found myself clinging to my last memories of him, even glancing at the phone like I'm waiting for his daily phone call."

"Sounds like you're being pulled in different directions."

"Did you consider leaving your profession when your wife died? To be more available to your children, perhaps?"

"I erred on the side of my profession at first . . . as a way to alleviate the hurt, I suppose. I wanted to separate myself from anything that would remind me of Reye. Including, unfortunately, even my children at times. I made sure they were taken care of, of course. They lived with their grandmothers while I returned to Cairo and my job without them. We needed to be together those first few weeks, and we weren't."

"But they're living with you now?"

"Yes. And I'm finding so much enjoyment in them. I think my daughter has forgiven me for that initial abandonment, or she never thought there was anything to forgive. We live on the same wavelength. But I wonder how much my son has forgiven me. He adored his mother." Mark shook his head. "Excuse me for rambling on. Your loss is much more recent than mine."

"But the fact that you've gone through it and are moving on with your life encourages me." Mark wondered if she were going to share more deeply, but she didn't. "I guess I should take a look at the report of death now."

She examined the document Mark handed her. Without comment, she put it in her folder. "Thank you. You've been very helpful."

She rose. "When my parents finish their business in Trois-Rivières in a couple of weeks, I'll travel with them to California for Bill's funeral. I plan to stay with them through the holidays and into the new year. I'll leave my parents' address there for you in case you need to contact me about anything while I'm there."

Mark rose. "Please do that." Was this the time to suggest a social meeting before she left for a long visit to California? While she waited for her parents to finish business dealings and visit friends? No, of course not. She was still grieving. "I'll walk you to the elevator."

When they reached the shiny metal door, he punched the button. "Shall I give you a call in a few days, to see how you're doing?"

Clair smiled. "I'd like that."

After she entered the elevator, Mark returned to the office. He sat at his desk, lost in thought, until Fern, his Canadian assistant, came in with a notarial for him to witness.

CHAPTER TEN

*M*ark was musing about Clair again when Olivier St. Arnoud phoned for a visit. They met in Mark's office.

"The death of William Ernest Bancroft is now officially being treated as a murder," Olivier said. "At this time, we cannot tie certain happenings in the area to the murder, but we have suspicions."

"Happenings?"

"What do you know about various anarchist movements to destroy governmental authority?"

Mark recalled his conversation with John Morris. "Until recently I would have associated them with Russia. Or Europe after World War II. Or a student movement in France that wanted to overturn the established order."

"What do you know of the student movements in your country and mine twenty or so years ago?"

"Anarchy wasn't well-known in my neck of the woods at the time. But due to Bancroft's death, I have given myself a crash course lately."

Olivier sighed. "It appears that a group is attempting to spread its message throughout North America. We believe that certain Americans from Northern California have attempted to join forces with Quebecois movements for separatism."

"A repeat of what you had in the seventies?"

"Not exactly. The people we are tracking now want to destroy all governments, not just a federal one here. They are trying to use the separatists, not join them. However, they will attempt to build a movement with or without them."

"Was Bancroft involved in this movement in California?"

"If they killed him, as we suspect, he was obviously some kind of threat to them. Perhaps he was an idealist, wishing to quietly encourage certain philosophic thinking but not interested in anything like insurrection."

"Why would they perceive him as a threat?"

"Perhaps he feared that the movement was going too far. He appears sincerely motivated to work for a better society, but perhaps he found himself in a more deadly group, going further than he wished. They may have feared he could become conscience-stricken and go to the police with names."

Mark remembered Clair saying her husband wanted to escape any kind of violence. "You think someone from this West Coast anarchist movement may have killed him to prevent him from turning on them?"

"Something like that."

Mark cleared his throat. "Do you think Bancroft's wife could be in danger?"

"Depends on whether she knows the things that got her husband killed."

CHAPTER ELEVEN

*M*ark, who never found it easy to ask a woman to spend time with him, was surprised at how easily this third meeting with Clair fell into place when he called and asked if she'd like to get together with him at one of St. Lawrence's riverside parks on Saturday. He'd suggested they grab takeout, but she offered to bring sandwiches for both of them to eat.

This time Deedra and the twins didn't tease him. Perhaps they were already accepting his going out with a woman as a normal activity.

Mark picked Clair up at her apartment building. By the time he finished stowing an old-fashioned hamper and an ice chest into the trunk of the Voyager, she had slid into the front passenger seat, eliminating any hesitation about whether he should open the door for her. Was this courtesy a throwback to Mark's rural past?

As they drove toward the park, Mark asked, "Are your parents still here?"

"Yes, for a little while longer. They're tying up their business in Trois-Rivières. They also wanted to say a few prayers in the parish church where they were active before moving to the States."

"Bill never had religious views, I take it?"

She gazed out the window. "His mother had been a staunch Christian of the conservative variety. But Bill had no particular religious tradition.

He wasn't even an atheist. Organized religion didn't concern him enough to even talk about it—for or against."

"And you?" Mark dared ask.

She shrugged. "Catholic will do as well any other pigeonhole, I guess. I guess I have a Dorothy Day kind of mindset."

Mark searched his memory banks for what he knew about Dorothy Day, the American social activist. "She worked as a pacifist and a spokesperson for workers, right? After she converted to Catholicism, as I recall, she founded the Catholic Worker Movement."

"She wasn't really a socialist, but she did call herself an anarchist."

"A peaceful anarchist?"

Clair laughed. "I would call her both an anarchist and an anti-war protestor, so not a militant in the sense of wanting to foment military action. She's kind of a hero of mine. Perhaps it's one reason I haven't spurned my Catholic heritage."

They reached the park, green and shimmering in the warm sunshine. They set the hamper and ice chest in a grassy spot on a blanket Mark had brought along. He rolled up another one to serve as a backrest. As they sat cross-legged facing each other, Clair opened the cooler to reveal a couple of wine coolers and various soft drinks.

"I wasn't sure what you'd prefer. I know you're from the South. Some people in one of my college classes were from Alabama, and they were adamant about not drinking anything with alcohol. So I brought a selection of choices."

"Very thoughtful." He pulled out a can of cola, pulled back the top, then took a sip. "I grew up in a small mountain community. We teenagers got mixed signals about alcohol." He smiled at a memory. "One of my classmates apparently got drunk on mouthwash."

"Scandalous!" Clair giggled.

"The church I grew up in preached avoidance of anything with alcohol in it. But I heard rumors that a few of the church members frequented the bootleggers."

Her eyes widened. "What's a bootlegger?"

"Guess you haven't seen the Robert Mitchum movie *Thunder Road*, huh?" She shook her head. "Parts of it were filmed in the east Tennessee Appalachians, not far from where I grew up. At one time people called bootleggers brewed whiskey in stills hidden in isolated mountain hideouts in so-called dry counties in the US, mostly in the rural South. In our area at the time, the sale of alcohol was illegal. Even beer. The bootleggers supplied alcohol to those unwilling to give it up."

Clair set out paper plates and a bowl of salad. She followed with a plate of ham sandwiches.

After a few bites, he said, "This ham is great. Do I detect a taste of honey?"

She smiled. "From a Quebecois? No, that's maple syrup basting."

"Of course."

"Is this bootlegging still going on in your part of the United States?"

"Not much anymore, that I know of. My hometown, Mocking Bird, Georgia, went wet, as it's called, several years ago because of the tourist trade. Big fight over it. Bootleggers and churches against the businesspeople."

"It's hard for me to imagine."

"I accepted responsible social drinking as a fact of life long ago. But before my father gave up booze to marry my mother, he appeared to have real problems with alcohol. Unable to stop with just one drink. Some of it may have been because of experiences he had in World War II. Because of his worry that I might've inherited some kind of predisposition, he asked me not to risk it. Not drinking at all ensures I'll never have to worry about becoming an alcoholic."

"Will you ask your children never to drink too?"

"Not planning to. Their grandfather died when they were young of cancer, not alcoholism. He never got near alcohol after he married my mother. I suppose I'll mention the possibility of an alcoholic inclination lurking in their makeup. Mainly I hope they'll see the virtue of moderation in all of life." He winked at her. "Have I spilled more personal history than you wanted to hear?"

Her delightful laugh eased his doubts. "You've painted a picture of a loving relationship between a son and his father."

"Don't suppose you'd give me the recipe for this salad."

"You like to cook?"

"I do, especially on weekends."

"You share meal preparation with your mother?"

"She does most of it during the week. I do my thing on the weekends. We share the household responsibilities ... just like I did with my wife, Reye."

"Did she have a job?"

"I took off a couple of years when the twins were little so she could go back to work."

"Were you both diplomats?"

He laughed. "I'm not actually a diplomat. Just a lowly consular officer—giving visas and helping American citizens in trouble. No high-level meetings with world leaders or that sort of thing."

"Isn't it unusual, given your profession, to go on a long leave like you did when your children were small?"

"Yes. We had to maneuver a bit to make it happen."

"It appears that you are not the overbearing diplomat—forcing wars and your will on the world at large."

"That's your image of what I do for a living?"

"Well, I do think the United States has been a bit of a bully in some respects." Her playful smile hinted that she was baiting him. "It often seems to act condescendingly toward smaller nations."

Choosing not to take the bait, Mark stretched out on his back, careful not to encroach on Clair's personal space. He rested his head on clasped hands over the rolled-up blanket. "My father wanted me to be a missionary. He was a Marine in World War II and survived island-hopping in the Pacific. I think he figured that as a missionary, I could redeem some of the killing he was a part of during that war."

"But you didn't follow that path?"

"I felt called to serve my country by helping people the way my job does instead." Mark raised up on one elbow and faced Clair. "What's your story?"

She gazed at the puffy white clouds in the pale-blue sky. "I grew up in a typical upper-middle-class family. Lived in California with Catholic parents and an older brother. My father was an accountant. My mother was active in church and school groups. In my early teens, I became bored with church. I didn't openly rebel, but I couldn't wait to graduate from high school and find my own way in college. I went to San Jose State."

"Is that where you met Bill?"

An uncomfortable silence followed. "It was a gradual thing. We lived in a . . . communal-type arrangement."

What did that mean? He was afraid to ask.

She watched a couple bicycling down the St. Lawrence bike path. "I was really mixed up with the heady anti-war movement, so sure we were going to create a new world. And we thought we knew how to carry it out." She shook her head. "So naïve."

Mark waited for her to tell him what blew apart their happy world.

She sat up and turned to face him. "The guy who led our group was quite a charmer. Rooney conjured up an exciting image of this better world we would make." She stumbled on, ejecting thoughts like ripping off a scab from a wound. "He seemed so dedicated to getting rid of war." She stared into her lap. "I fell in love with him."

Was she deciding how specific to be in recounting her experiences? How specific did he really want her to be?

"Lots of things went on during that time that I'm not proud of. But . . ." A troubled look crossed her face. "Rooney and I became . . . partners. Soon after that, I began to see his ruthless side."

"Did he hurt you?"

"No. But one time he started to beat up a guy who had the gall to talk back to him at one of the protests. A couple of other men pulled Rooney off. If they hadn't, I think he would have killed the man."

Could Rooney have gone from *almost* to murder?

"I hated what he had become. But I hid it well. He never suspected. Together we visited groups in various places to recruit them. I met Bill Bancroft on one of those trips. He seemed solid. Good. We began to see each other secretly whenever Rooney was away."

She picked up a napkin and toyed with it. "Long story short, Bill and I left the group. We married, with just my family present."

She hesitated so long that Mark wondered if she was struggling with what the church called "unconfessed sin."

"After we married, I applied for landed immigrant status for Bill, and we came here."

Her abrupt finish told him she had left out large segments of their lives, but he didn't press for details.

"When Bill and I started having difficulties, we separated. And I occasionally attended a Quaker gathering." She smiled. "Guess I was searching for something solid and wholesome."

After resting a few minutes in the summer sun, they stowed blankets and picnic remains in the Voyager's trunk and walked up the pathway by the river, listening to the breeze stir the leaves.

Mark shared how he and Reye had met in an orientation class for the Foreign Service.

"Were you happy to have twins?" she asked.

"I admit to being a bit floored at first. Reye took it much better than I did. But now I couldn't imagine it any other way."

"Treat your children with care," Clair said. "You are so fortunate to have them." She looked away.

He sensed an ache in her heart concerning kids and wanted to ask but decided to let her share such intimate details in her own time.

They halted when the path took a turn away from the river. Clair faced Mark. "Thank you so much for today. For the first time since Bill's death, I feel like I've taken a step outside the grief."

"I'm glad." Mark took her hand. "What are your plans for the future?"

"I'm going to visit my family in California through the beginning of the new year. Probably eventually move to California, because of family and friends."

He felt a clenching in his gut and hoped she didn't notice. "Think you'll stick around here for a while first?"

"I have to. My lease on the apartment runs through early summer, and Bill's lease on the bookstore ends shortly after. Right now, the couple who run a print shop next door are keeping it open a few hours during the week. It's in a pretty isolated neighborhood. Just a few small specialty operations. I don't know why Bill picked that area, except that it was cheap. I'll need to either hire someone to keep it open full time or close it and sell it."

Clearly she had mixed feelings about both options. How attached did she remain to the memory of her seemingly absent-minded husband?

When they reached her complex, Mark pulled into the only close parking spot, a ten-minute loading zone, and helped her carry the hamper and ice chest up to her apartment.

"I'm going to stay with my parents for a while. Can I call you when I get back?"

"Please do."

The door closed lightly behind him.

On the way home, Mark fought melancholy by planning the future. While Clair was in California, maybe she'd have time to process the grief over her husband's death. He would have time himself as well, for the idea hatching in his brain to grow into hope for something he had no right to expect. Perhaps after she came back, he might mention to her how often overseas schools needed teachers.

CHAPTER TWELVE

The hint of changing seasons lent a precariousness to this outdoor meeting. Mark had met John on the bench close to McGill University. But soon this brilliantly sunny day would yield to lower temperatures, and future meetings would have to be held indoors, probably in the Notre Dame complex.

A conglomerate of office workers, university students, middle-aged women, and a few of the city's homeless strolled, talked, and took advantage of the balmy weather.

"No doubt about it, I'm attracted to her," Mark mused after spilling his guts about Clair. "It's certainly not love at this point. And certainly not an affair. I just really enjoy having a friendship with an intelligent woman. Like I had with Reye."

"The best relationships begin that way," John said. "Of course, it could become something more."

"I know. But Clair's from such a different background than Reye."

"Are you worried about having to give up your career if your relationship grows?"

Mark stretched out his legs in front of him, noticing a worn spot on one of the trouser knees. He really needed some new clothes. "I wouldn't want to give up my career for marriage. But I don't think that's in danger."

And yet, only a few weeks ago, hadn't he wondered if he should give up the Foreign Service so the twins could have a more permanent home?

He checked his watch. "If you have a bit more time, I'd like to talk more about civil disorder and anarchism."

John grinned at the sudden change of subject. "I've cleared the early afternoon for you. We can talk about whatever you want."

"I appreciate that."

He hadn't laid out for John the details of the death that led him to Clair. "One of the cases I'm involved in concerns an American who died in suspicious circumstances. The evidence is strong that an anarchist group may be involved."

"Really?" His eyes sparked with interest.

"I'm grateful for democratically elected leaders. I don't understand why anyone would want to destroy democracy."

John looked away for a moment. "Canada has given refuge to many groups of Americans for various reasons. From the royalists who didn't want to fight King George to the young men who thought the US had no business getting involved in the Vietnamese conflict. Not to mention the American Blacks who fled slavery."

Mark sighed. "Blacks in my country continue to suffer from discrimination." He came from Appalachian poor. No slave owners in his ancestry. Nevertheless, he was white.

"I thought the civil rights movement made changes for the better," John said.

"It definitely did. But the effects of discrimination linger on. And not just for Blacks. Poor whites in the Appalachians suffer poverty because of coal mining and less access to good schools. And yet, it seems to me that rich white kids are more likely to go for anarchy than poor black ones— or poor white ones, for that matter."

"You're saying anarchy is more of a middle-class kind of rebellion?"

"Or maybe of certain educated folks, both black and white. Bad things can happen when the majority rule. I certainly don't want rule by the minority either. But sometimes what the majority wants is wrong."

John shook his head. "Can't disagree with that."

"Southern whites didn't want their former slaves voting, so they passed laws making it hard for Blacks to vote."

"But just because the majority wants something doesn't mean that what they want is just."

"When you think the majority is in error," Mark said, "you have to be careful that the cure isn't worse than the illness."

"You can make a choice against the destroying kind of anarchy, the kind that results in civil disobedience. You don't force or destroy anything. You witness."

"I like that idea."

John stared into space. "Some of what was going on in the sixties was nonviolent witnessing. But some was pure destruction. It's easy for destroyers to take over a peaceful protest."

A perfect example of Rooney Steiger, Mark supposed. Had he killed someone?

And was Clair hiding his secret and carrying a load of guilt?

CHAPTER THIRTEEN

*M*onique Martel called Mark at work and invited him to "a small dinner party in my apartment this weekend." Her voice breathed uncomplicated cheer.

His introverted nature grasped at Monique's lifeline that might pull him from his depression. He'd been spending far too much time moping about Clair. "I'd love to."

His family gave him the third degree when they found out he was going to see the woman he'd dated before the one who'd lost her husband.

"Did you break up with Clair?" Deedee asked.

"Clair's just a friend, sweetie. And she's out of town right now."

"So you're playing around?" Sean asked.

What part of *just a friend* didn't they get?

Nevertheless, the thought of his family waiting to grill him the next day would likely save him from actions he would seriously have regretted later.

Monique's gathering was small, with just two other couples—one married, one not. Mark wasn't sure about the status of the second couple. Were they live-in partners? Close friends? The party was bilingual, freely switching from Quebecois French to English and back again.

During the meal of beef and vegetables, the others conversed about who had traveled where this past summer. They nodded politely when Mark responded to queries about his career and places he had lived. Shortly after dessert, both couples left, saying they had a theatre engagement.

When Mark rose to leave as well, Monique placed a hand on his arm. "I want to know more about those countries you lived in and your exciting life."

Her feminine touch stirred his newly awakened hunger, and he sat with her on the couch and talked. As they sipped on their drinks, he felt stirrings he hadn't experienced since before Reye died.

"How about we continue this in my bedroom," she murmured.

As though his guardian angel were keeping watch, a vision flashed in his mind: the thought of entering his home after an assignation with Monique, with his family and his dead father staring at him with disappointment.

Son, Drayton Pacer said, *being with a woman feels good.* As his father knew from experience. *But do you really want the kind of relationship where you both selfishly get whatever you want? Aren't you really looking for a lifelong partnership with a woman, maybe with more children to come?*

Monique's mouth turned down in a pout. "You're not gay, are you?"

"Definitely not." He rose and headed for the door.

She remained on the couch. "This is it for us, then?"

He felt like he was in a scene from some B-grade movie. "Yes, it is."

When the door shut behind him, he inhaled a cleansing breath.

CHAPTER FOURTEEN

*M*ark arrived home from work early for a change. The twins were playing a game with some neighbor children in the combined yards. He waved at them as he entered the house.

His mother sat in the living room, staring into space. No smells of food wafted from the kitchen.

"Mama?"

She startled. "Mark!" She glanced at the clock. "Goodness. I need to start supper. Guess I'll pull out leftovers."

She stood, but Mark touched her arm. "What's wrong?"

Deedra slumped back on the couch. "The doctor called with the results from that annual physical I had last week."

His heart sank. "What did he say?"

"One of the tests came back showing a growth of some sort in my uterus. He wants me to have an operation—perhaps a hysterectomy if cancer is found."

The C word. Cancer had killed his father. But that was related to his heavy smoking, wasn't it? His mother had done nothing to bring on something like this.

He tried to sound calm. "You should have the operation as soon as possible. The sooner we know, the sooner it can be treated. Right?"

Deedra wrung her hands. "I guess I could ask Melba to stay with the children for a few days. I just don't want to upset the children."

"If we're calm, they'll take it calmly. Let's get the date set up, work things out with Melba, then tell them."

"Okay." She rose. "Let me go pull out those leftovers. The children will be getting hungry."

Ignoring his own feelings of dread, Mark kept up the casual conversation during supper. After they had cleared the dishes and the children had left for baths and homework, he and his mother discussed plans. The quiet around them, normally a blessing, now felt oppressive.

"I'll call Dr. Tauber tomorrow," Deedra said. Then she left for her room . . . to pray and read the Bible, no doubt.

Melba would do what was needed, if called on, but she didn't like leaving home. If, God forbid, his mother was taken, Melba would push for raising the children in Forest Plains.

As he prepared for bed, his thoughts turned to God—with a touch of bitterness. "I did the right thing, despite Monique's tempting. And You sent *this*?"

CHAPTER FIFTEEN

While Deedra was at Dr. Tauber's office for a final consultation a few days before the planned operation, Mark sat the twins down in the living room. "Grandmom Melba's coming for a visit. She wants to see us before the weather changes. While she's here, Grandmom Deedra is going into the hospital for a couple of days for a little operation."

The silence from the twins told him they were past the stage of being fooled by Mark's attempt to sugarcoat the process.

"Dad," Sean said, "is Grandmom Deedra going to die?"

"Well, we're all going to die someday."

Sean sighed like a parent with a stubborn child. "I mean, is she going to die from whatever she's going to the hospital for?"

"I don't know. She has cancer. But we don't know yet how serious it is." Sean tensed.

Deedee had been the last to see her mother alive, talk with her, be held by her. "We'll help Grandmom Melba with the cooking and stuff."

Quite a gift, since Deedee was not drawn to anything to do with the kitchen.

He hugged both of his children and did his best to assure them that whatever happened, they'd all be okay.

• • • • •

Melba fell easily into the family routine. Deedra and Melba's relationship had always been more like sisters than in-laws.

The twins rebelled when Mark told them they had to attend school on the day of the operation.

"If you won't let us wait with you at the hospital, we'll run away and walk there," Deedee said.

"The hospital doesn't allow visitors under thirteen," Mark pointed out.

"I can stay home with Sean and Deedee," Melba said. "They'll be much better here than fidgeting and worrying through a school day. You can call as soon as you find out how the operation went."

He yielded, as he seemed to do often these days.

• • • • •

For the first time in his life, Mark sat in a hospital waiting room while a loved one endured a major operation. He thought of Reye's death: sudden, wrenchingly unexpected—yet, mercifully, with little suffering. His father had died in his living room chair, the newspaper on his lap. An older relative or two had died after a time of suffering, but most members of his family tended toward a healthy old age. The thought of one he loved suffering a long, perhaps painful illness called him into new territory.

He frequently used a pay phone to check in with Melba and the twins. During the calls, Melba tried to offer comfort, but she knew illness didn't always have a happy ending.

"Your mother's a strong woman. You know she's not worried about herself. And she told me last night that she has left the children to God and she's at peace no matter what happens."

The churning in Mark's gut quieted a bit.

"You have to be strong for her."

He didn't know how.

After seemingly hours of turning tattered magazine pages, Mark saw Dr. Tauber coming toward him, still in his scrubs. He tried to gauge from the doctor's demeanor if the operation was successful, but his expression was maddeningly neutral.

He nodded at Mark. "We think we got it all."

Think? Mark wished for something more definitive.

"I see no evidence of metastasizing. We'll talk to your mother later about follow-up treatments, but for the moment she's resting comfortably. The nurse will let you know when you can see her."

Mark thanked him and then phoned the family, delivering it as good news. But what would follow-up treatment involve? Cancer, heart attacks, and the other serious ailments, especially when they came to people later in life, sometimes were accompanied by debilitating treatments.

And his mother would have a mountain woman's disdain for any prolonged treatment that prevented her from carrying out her normal activities.

CHAPTER SIXTEEN

As Mark had suspected, Deedra adamantly refused radiation therapy. "Not at my age. I saw what it did to my sister, and she died anyway. An operation is one thing. Having life slowly sapped out of you is something else."

They didn't discuss it when the twins were around. Sean and Deedee seemed to have made it through the crisis, assuming that because the operation was deemed a success, everything was back to normal.

"Daddy didn't choose any massive treatment," Mark said, wanting to support her. "I guess, for him, that was the right choice."

Melba made it clear she would've chosen the radiation treatments. But the choice, obviously, was Deedra's to make. And Melba agreed to support her decision.

Not wanting anyone to second-guess her choice, Deedra showed a renewed interest in life. She tried new recipes and sewed new curtains. She got back her job of tutoring college students in English as a second language one afternoon a week.

As Melba prepared to leave for Forest Plains, the adults sat around the dinner table and discussed when they'd see each other again. "Why don't you come see me before winter sets in?" she suggested.

Before Clair came into his life, Mark had yearned for a trip to Mocking Bird. It was his home after all. Might be for his children too.

Deedra put down her coffee cup. "Mark, when is Thanksgiving here in Canada?"

"The tenth of October this year. I could request some time off. Things start to slow down in the fall. We could visit the Adirondacks, maybe make a side trip to the Maine coast, Acadia National Park, then a few days in Forest Plains." Like most Foreign Service officers, he had plenty of unused vacation time.

His mother peered into her coffee cup. "I haven't been back home in quite a while." No doubt where home was for her. She told everyone that Mocking Bird was her home "until I reach my heavenly one."

Mark touched her hand. "I'd like to introduce the twins to where you were raised. Last time they were there they weren't old enough to really get the taste of it."

In addition, the trip would help pass the time for him as he waited for Clair to return. A trip to Mocking Bird, and touching base with his childhood home again, would hopefully lead him out of his floundering for meaning and purpose.

CHAPTER SEVENTEEN

*M*ark told the twins' teacher he wanted to take them out of school over the Thanksgiving break to make a trip to their home in the States. "Would it be a problem if we extended it a couple of weeks?"

"Not at all," the teacher assured him. The twins were excellent students. She arranged for them to be given assignments to keep up with their classes. "Being with their families will be good for them."

While preparing for the trip, thoughts of Clair intruded. What was she doing? Enjoying her family, no doubt. Was she going to move back to California? Was she haunted by fears of harm coming to her there? Or here?

How about his own future? He had to live in a country like the US or Canada that had the health services his mother needed. Would he consider a permanent move stateside? Taking a civil service job with the State Department maybe?

On a clear October day with the barest hint of winter, the family packed up and headed south. On highway 15, they crossed the familiar St. Lawrence out of Montreal and then the border into New York State. The highway became US I-87, mileage signs replacing those marking kilometers.

South on I-87, then west on I-90, with a quick stop for lunch at a McDonald's. They stopped for the night at a Holiday Inn outside Cincinnati, Ohio.

The next day his mother did some of the driving as they crisscrossed Midwest farming country on various interstates. They crossed the Mississippi River into Missouri at St. Louis on I-70. In a couple of days, they would cross the river again to make their way to the south.

Continuing west, they followed state highways toward Forest Plains. The twins looked for recognizable landmarks as they neared the only American town they really knew. They cheered when they passed the Forest Plains town limits.

Mark pulled into the driveway of the familiar house, built for large families back in the twenties. The twins spilled out of the car and raced up the steps into Melba's arms.

Following hugs among the grown-ups, they unpacked and washed up. The smell of spiced ham and candied sweet potatoes and a host of other familiar dishes drew them to the table and an overflowing blessing to a merciful God.

Was it easier to find Him here, loosened from familiar and worrying routines?

Melba's small town was a second home to the twins—the only one that didn't change every two or three years.

Thoughts of Clair's trip "home" kept intruding on these reflections, no matter how hard he tried to suppress them.

· · · · ·

Mark and his family attended the Sunday service at Melba's church, then he and Deedra fellowshipped with Melba while the twins played with Laura and Jeff, the brother and sister they had made friends with last summer.

A few days later, Mark, Deedra, and the twins arose just after dawn and piled into the car, seasoned travelers now, looking forward to the journey. The twins were excited to see their father's home. Their enthusiasm for travel was an inheritance from both of their parents.

Perhaps the kids would see the town where he had lived for the first eighteen years of his life as just another foreign country. Their upbringing so eclipsed his. Wasn't his concern one reason for this trip? Could they even glimpse what it was like growing up in Mocking Bird, Georgia, in the 1960s?

They traveled southeast from Forest Plains through Missouri's boot hill to cross the Mississippi River into Tennessee just west of Dyersburg, located on the Forked Deer River.

This was west Tennessee, with its swamps and meandering rivers, a land strange to Mark though he had spent four years in a Tennessee college. His school, in the far eastern point of the state, home to the Smokies and other mountain ranges, was more familiar terrain to a boy raised in the north Georgia mountains.

They stopped at a riverside café for a meal of catfish fillets, accompanied by the cornmeal bread known as hush puppies, and slaw with bits of apple. Then they headed east by the southern Tennessee route through Savannah, Pulaski, and Fayetteville.

East of Chattanooga, they stopped for an early supper in a diner frequented by local families, the southern dialect of Mark's youth soft on his ears. They were on the eastern downside of the Cumberland mountains, the Appalachians still to the west.

In the early evening, they traveled into the north Georgia mountains and terrain Mark had once called home.

Growing tired, he gave the driving over to Deedra. Besides being fresh, she was more accustomed than Mark to the town he hadn't visited in years. After a dark descent through backroads, she maneuvered them to a motel that hadn't been there when Mark last visited.

A person can never be so lost as when they return years later to the place they knew in their childhood.

CHAPTER EIGHTEEN

The children woke early the next morning, after sleeping deeply all night. Their father's profession had accustomed them to traveling and to changes of scenery and places to live.

At the motel's common room, they breakfasted on sugar-coated cereal, donuts, and other delights seldom allowed at home.

Mark's college dorm marked the first time he had stayed in commercial lodging of any sort. The few trips his family took in his childhood were short ones to visit relatives, with whom they stayed for a night or two. His Foreign Service training opened his eyes to what appeared ultimate luxury accommodations. Now a seasoned world traveler, he still marveled at the amenities one enjoyed in a fairly modest hotel chain.

The last time he had come here was to bury his father. His mother had visited several times in the past few years. She valued family and place. What had he lost? What had his children lost?

"You'll be surprised at how things have changed," Deedra said. "Every time I come, there's a new subdivision or a new store in the shopping center."

She allowed the buffet hostess to refill her coffee cup, continuing the conversation after thanking her. "Are you going to let Jeremy show you around before we get together with the family tonight?" She planned to spend most of the day with her cousin Buck and his family. They were all going to get together at their place tonight to renew old family connections.

"I think the twins and I will mosey around town this morning, take in the sights. Find all those new places you've talked about. Probably take the twins to Jeremy's store this afternoon." Mark hadn't warned Jeremy that he would be visiting. But apparently word had passed from Mark's relatives to him. Would he find their friendship hadn't stood the test of the long absence of letters between them?

"Try to stop by the church while you're out. It's beautiful. Somebody donated a big piece of forest land to them so they could construct a new building. The rest of the acreage has to stay open to public use. Some group has built trails on it."

The service for his father had taken place in the newly established church, a rebuilt structure that used to house the post office. The twins were just a few months old.

This town might as well be a new Foreign Service posting for the family. Even the regional English was steeped in different accents and expressions. His own voice, he realized, had taken a slight tilt toward his childhood mountain drawl since they arrived here.

Deedra planned to ask Buck to take her to visit a few older relatives. Then she'd join his family and help with preparations for tonight's gathering. She would meet Mark and the twins back at the motel, she said, sometime in the late afternoon to freshen up for the evening. That way Mark and the children would have the car all day.

Eventually Mark would need Jeremy's address. Like most people in the town, he no longer picked up his mail from a post office box.

Before their visit, Deedra had written to Buck about their plans. He had answered and enclosed a short note from Jeremy, practically whooping with delight that their two families could finally get together. *Come see me*, he wrote, *as soon as you get into town.* They'd planned to spend lots of time at his and Lee Ann's place with their children.

Mark felt himself drawn into a whirlwind of activities he wasn't sure he was ready for. He needed time to psych himself up for them.

• • • • •

The clapboard church had vanished and the surrounding area covered with an upscale housing development. He recalled the breathtaking view from the old church of the mountains, back when views were cheap.

He nursed a Rip Van Winkle disbelief. Right here—on this flat with the creek that caught the runoff—had been the slapped-together parsonage where Abigail Childress lived with her overly strict parents. Were tiny automobile parts still buried beneath the surface from the three or four derelict vehicles that always decorated the yard?

The buildings had been cleared, the creek turned into a meandering stream with a walkway, and big houses constructed farther down on the other side. A different kind of neighborhood from the low-income one scattered around then, some inhabitants trying to do a little farming in the small fields.

What had happened to Abigail? Had she managed to escape her past? What about her child? And the football captain, whose name he couldn't remember, responsible as much as she for the child but not called to face the consequences.

He was glad women in Abigail's situation weren't as shamed now, but he hurt for all the babies who didn't know their fathers. He had dealt with such a son a few years ago in his job at the US consulate in Jeddah. The man, from the Philippines, was trying to prove that the man he believed had sired him was an American citizen and thus able to pass citizenship to his son.

The man said he'd found his father, but the man refused to acknowledge him as his son. He had a wife and family now and an important job with some hot-shot company.

Deedee brought him back to the present. "I guess it must have been a small church," she said, staring at the former location. "Was it in a house?"

The twins had worshipped in a home church in one of their overseas sojourns as well as in a larger, more ancient Egyptian Christian church. In their upbringing, churches, like schools, came in different shapes and sizes and orders of worship.

"No, it was a building, but a small one, with a fellowship room off to one side."

Mark was glad the church of his childhood no longer existed. He hoped the church Jeremy now attended knew something of the love Jesus had championed.

He and the twins took slow steps over the creek on the pedestrian bridge and past the manicured lawn of the first house in the development. A man standing in front of a three-car garage stared at them as they passed, reluctantly returning Mark's wave.

After passing a few more houses, Mark led them back over the bridge to where their car was parked. "What do you say we go look at the town where I grew up?"

He'd psyched himself up as much as he was going to.

CHAPTER NINETEEN

The old town center had not only survived but thrived, despite the shopping complex, which his mother had said was farther out on the highway. Trendy shops and restaurants, as well as at least one boutique bed-and-breakfast, proclaimed a new era. The old drugstore with lunch counter had been remodeled with a much larger eating space.

"When can we eat, Dad?" Sean asked.

"You ate enough to feed Cox's army at the motel just a couple of hours ago."

"A snack then? From the drugstore?"

"Let's wait until we've explored a little more."

Mocking Bird had not died, as had so many American small towns, nor had it become a bedroom community for the closest metropolitan area, in this case Atlanta. Mocking Bird had the good fortune to find itself in a happy medium. It was too far away from the big city for a daily commute—for most, at least. But it was close enough to Atlanta for retirees who still wanted an occasional visit. Weekend visitors up for a weekend in the mountains made up the other population segment for the town's retail areas. Now a retirement/tourist town, it allowed locals to remain and thrive in it, especially entrepreneurial types like Jeremy.

They found a parking space near a bookstore, which had not been there in Mark's childhood. Neither he nor his children could pass up a bookstore, given time to explore.

They entered and found their way to a large children's section. Mark bought a book for each of the twins: *The Boy Who Harnessed the Wind* by William Kamkwamba for Sean, *Death on the Nile* by Agatha Christie for Deedee, who had recently discovered the British author.

Out on the street again, Mark couldn't resist leading them for a quick tour of the library, in the same spot as the old one but expanded into a larger building. Inside, Mark gestured to the small children's library, where he had spent much time when he was the twins' age.

"This small alcove was the whole library when I was growing up," he told them.

They nodded, tolerant of his diatribes about how much better the younger generation had it today.

At least they had inherited their parents' love of books. They headed for the children's fiction section to examine the treasures.

"We can't check them out, of course," Deedee sighed, paging through a Nancy Drew collection, possibly left over from Mark's time as a child.

He remembered the librarian of his youth, an older lady named Francine Lewis. Mark owed a great deal to the woman who had helped a small boy quench his thirst for learning about the world beyond Mocking Bird.

On the street again, Mark studied the mix of pedestrians, mostly tourists. Older citizens, some stylishly dressed, others less so, including one man in overalls.

Sean gazed up at him. "Can we eat *now*?"

They strolled to the drugstore, where Mark got a BLT, hamburgers for Deedee and Sean.

Out on the street again, Mark led them to the end of the business district, where Jeremy ran the hardware store. The old brick building looked just like the original downtown hardware store begun by Jeremy's grandfather. The front display window had been enlarged to show a fancy riding lawn mower and other gas-powered yard equipment. The twins studied the small arrangement of games, along with normal hardware items, many of which had not been invented when the store began.

"Can we go inside, Daddy?" Deedee asked.

"I think we'll come back later. I want to do some exploring first."

The kids acquiesced and hiked back to the car.

Why was he delaying a meeting with the best friend of his childhood? Was he afraid Jeremy had changed from the boy he used to go to the old drugstore with to watch girls? Or did he envy Jeremy for choosing to stay in this strange yet heart-familiar place?

Was he afraid he might be tempted to return?

CHAPTER TWENTY

The sign in front of the church on the edge of town beckoned. Mark took the car down the gravel drive past an open gate onto the grounds of the forested preserve. The mature trees surely were left from a time before the church was built.

Mark parked in the lot behind the church. The twins tumbled out, and he followed.

He studied the newish structure before them, a low-level building of mellow brick, umber and russet, interspersed with windows of colored glass framed in dark wood. Modest, not showy. He figured the sanctuary would hold several hundred worshippers.

A couple on the far side of the grounds emerged from what appeared to be a hiking trail.

"I wish we could go to a church like this," Deedee said, "where we could hike and stuff."

Sean turned at the sound of a car parking behind them. "Who's that?" he asked in a low voice.

Mark turned to see a man and two young girls getting out of a late-model Acura. One of the girls looked about Sean's age, the other several years older.

Jeremy. Not as thin as Mark remembered him, a few creases in his face now and sporting a receding hairline, clad in jeans and a sport shirt.

He hastened toward Mark. "As I live and breathe. The dead do come back to life! How are you, Mark?"

They embraced briefly, patting each other's backs. "It's been a while," Mark said. "But time's been good to you, Jer."

"Might say the same about you. You don't look any different from the day we graduated from high school. Kept all your hair even. These two your offspring?"

"Yep. And those are yours, I guess."

"My name's Belle," the older girl said. "This is my sister, Janelle. What's y'all's names?"

"I'm Deedee. This is Sean."

Sean, seemingly struck dumb at the sight of a pretty girl his age, smiled weakly. The younger girl smiled back. All the children shook hands.

"Come on," Belle said. "We'll show you the playground while the grown-ups talk."

The four children took off.

Mark turned to his friend. "Still running your old man's store?"

"Sure am. A couple of 'em, actually. Opened a second one in the new shopping center. Listen, I'm sorry we didn't know about Reye's passing in time to go to her funeral. I didn't even have your address to write you. So sorry for your loss."

Mark swallowed. "Thanks. Yeah, we need to start writing each other again."

"Well, I'm glad you're here. Let me show you around our church." Jeremy led the way toward the door to the sanctuary. "I'm heading a study course for a group of close friends. I'll introduce you to the pastor in a bit, but first let's look at the auditorium." He opened the door, allowing Mark to enter first.

The tinted windows unfolded a rainbow of colors from the early-afternoon sun onto the pews. The impression was of a hushed forest due to the wood paneling and simple wooden pews cushioned in dark green. The pulpit was not raised, but the floor sloped slightly toward it.

"We built it and most of the furniture ourselves," Jeremy said as they settled onto one of the benches close to the front. "Didn't want to wrap ourselves in debt for fancy trappings. We've got a sister church in Nigeria we contribute to. We'd rather our money go for things like that."

"Not something our old church would have been interested in."

"Probably would have condemned even." He scowled momentarily, but his face quickly softened. "Your son's beginning to look like your dad. Sean, right?"

"We named him Sean Drayton for both grandfathers. He does resemble my daddy a lot—going to be taller than me, too, I think."

"I miss your dad. He didn't have much time here. But he made up for lost time while he lived."

"I guess he did."

"There was so much love in your house, Mark. I always liked going over there. I know now that my father loved me, in his own way. He just didn't know how to show it after Mama died."

"They did the best they could."

A young man entered, carrying a vase of flowers. "Okay if I come in?"

Jeremy waved him inside. "We're just palavering, JB. You got new flowers for the sanctuary?"

JB held out the vase like an offering. The names of the flowers came to Mark: pansies, snapdragon, viola. "My mother used to grow those."

The young man seemed overwhelmed by the slight praise, and Mark realized he had Down syndrome.

"JB has a real talent for flowers," Jeremy said. "Every few days, even if it's below freezing, he shows up with something pretty—dried flowers if nothing's blooming. Go ahead and put them on the altar, JB, so we can all admire them."

Beaming like a celebrity who'd just won an Oscar, JB obeyed, taking a moment for a last arranging. "I like flowers. They always listen to me."

He left without a backward glance, perhaps sensing that the two men wanted to talk.

"Our pastor's son," Jeremy said. "He's one of the most loved children in the world. And gives back every bit of it. He's great with the little ones. Helps the janitor too. We're lucky to have him."

"Jer, whatever happened to Abigail Childress?"

"I don't know. Her family hung on for a bit, while the church sort of came down around their ears. One night it literally burned to the ground, including the preacher's house. They all got out. After that they moved on. Don't know where." He shifted. "How long y'all going to be here?"

"A few days. We go back next Saturday."

"Well, we'll have all of you out for supper at our house. Tonight?"

"We're scheduled with my mom's folks."

"Tomorrow night then."

"Sounds good."

"Okay. Now, let me introduce you to our pastor."

They got up, passed through the doors where JB had exited, and walked a short distance down the hall to a room labeled "Pastor Jean."

Jean?

Jeremy knocked on the open door. "Pastor Jean? Can we disturb you for a bit?"

Mark managed not to do a double take when a woman, perhaps in her early forties, came out of the inner office. Petite, with short dark hair, she wore raspberry-colored slacks and a matching checkered blouse.

"You know you're not disturbing me." She held out her hand to Mark. "Jean Metcalf. You're Jeremy's friend?" Her accent was mid-South, not Appalachian.

They shook hands. "Mark Pacer. Jeremy and I grew up together."

90

"Welcome." Jean gestured toward several cushioned chairs in a small semicircle on one side of the office. They faced a window looking out on a grove of trees. Beside the grove was the playground where their four children were climbing on the jungle gym.

Jean pulled up a chair across from them. "Jeremy has shared about growing up with your family. I'm sorry I missed knowing your father. He's fondly remembered here by many of the members."

The woman's warmth awakened an unexpected desire to talk. "My father was a US Marine in the Pacific during World War II. I only realized later what a rapidly changing world he and the others came back to from the one they left."

Jean leaned forward, indicating interest in his story, so he continued. "He wanted to become a missionary, to make up for some of the killing and the horror. Unfortunately, his circumstances didn't allow it. Guess he kinda bequeathed that to me."

Jean smiled. "I thought Jeremy said you're a diplomat."

"I am," Mark hastened to explain. "But sometimes I feel a little like a missionary."

Jeremy laughed. "Your daddy was disappointed when you became a diplomat instead of going into mission work, but he came around and was really proud of you."

Mark glanced at his friend. "I owe a lot to you for being with him during those times when we . . . had our difficulties."

Jean sat back. "So he finally accepted your call toward a secular ministry?"

"I like that term," Mark said. "In my job as a consular officer, I spend a lot of time dealing with problems of Americans overseas. Child custody cases, for example. Recently, even a murder case."

Jean gasped. "Murder?"

Mark wished he hadn't thrown out the word so casually. "It appears an American citizen was deliberately killed in a hit-and-run."

"Interesting," Jean said.

"When I was growing up here, the rest of the world seemed remote. Until my teenage years, when Jeremy and I had to sign up for the draft. Even then, we were mostly concerned about how well the apple orchards were doing and whether the new superhighway would bring us more visitors." He shrugged. "I suppose even now movements like anarchism are still pretty unknown here."

She and Jeremy exchanged glances. "Interesting you would mention that," she said. "We had a shootout a while back. Are you familiar with Barnum Gap?"

"Sure. Daddy and I occasionally drove up an old road over there, then hiked up to the gap. Old-timers talked about the bootleggers who used to hang out around there." He didn't mention that his father may have tasted their products in his younger years. "All overgrown last time we were there years ago."

Jeremy took up the story. "Probably not too long after your last trip, some group took up residence there, but not to bootleg. Turns out they were hiding out after killing an FBI agent farther north—West Virginia, I think. The FBI laid siege. Different stories about what happened swarmed around, but their cabin burned to the ground. Probably self-inflicted, like they set the place on fire before all of 'em committed suicide."

"It happened just after I got here," Jean said. "Nobody local was involved, but it sure caused a stir for a while. We've been pretty quiet since then as far as anything like anarchy is concerned. Although we do have the farm out toward Rainy Mountain."

"A farm?"

Jeremy grinned. "Remember Old Man Keaton and his kin? Bunch of hippies joined the remnants of that group. It's sort of died down the last few years, though."

"I remember Keaton's farm. He was wounded in World War I, but he grew up here and was a military vet. People overlooked that he lived with more than one common-law wife and had a pack of kids."

"It was a commune, for sure."

"Different sorts of communal groups have been around for centuries," Jean said, "here and in the rest of the country. All over the world, for that matter. I studied them in a course at seminary. Some, like a few groups in the Middle Ages, only wanted to live peaceful lives, sharing property, but were persecuted anyway. More recently, the Soviet version under Stalin has been deadly for many people."

Like Bill Bancroft. "What do you think about those movements in the '70s, like the Haight-Ashbury hippies?"

Jean looked out the window. "The difference between trying to change society peacefully and advocating harmful methods to change it seems to be a dividing line."

"We don't usually have these kinds of discussions much around Mocking Bird." Jeremy chuckled.

"True," Jean agreed. "Our problems are the same ones most of the nation has. Drug use among some of our young people. Single parents struggling to raise their children. Older people dealing with lack of purpose now that they no longer have jobs."

"And this church is involved in these struggles?"

Jeremy nodded somberly. "Jean's a single parent."

"I was a highly paid executive on my way up. Made the mistake of sleeping with the boss."

Mark tried to hide his shock.

"I got careless, and the inevitable happened."

"JB?" he guessed.

She nodded. "I would've had an abortion, except that my parents stood by me. Told me to keep their grandchild alive, even when we knew he would be born with problems."

Jean must have told this story often, but her voice still trembled. "JB has been such a blessing. It's a long story that I won't take time for now, but I eventually found this calling, which I dearly love."

Did you truly have a calling?

CHAPTER TWENTY-ONE

The family gathering at Buck's began with casual conversation in the living room, mostly the men and children. The women gathered in the kitchen to visit and fix the meal, still following the traditional customs of Mark's youth.

A remembrance stung him for a brief moment of the countless meals he and Reye had enjoyed with overseas colleagues in their foreign postings, the men and women sharing not only conversation but also tasks.

Mark recognized most of the adults from his childhood days— cousins of his mother and their families. This was a Crockett family gathering.

His father's relatives were never as close as his mother's. No enmity that Mark knew of. His kin just weren't gatherers like hers were. Many of his father's family had left for jobs in other places, but few of his mother's had. Of course, his mother's folks were more well off and owned land.

He had left too, for college. He didn't know any of his father's relatives who had much of an education. His mother had planned to but didn't have the money.

Tonight his children and the other younger family members were taken in by the older ones. They migrated outside for various games that Mark remembered playing as a child: Sling the Statue and Mother, May I.

No alcohol or appetizers were served.

Various adult relations offered various renditions of scolding for Mark's having been away too long.

Buck began more serious conversation around the dining table as they passed the ham and biscuits and red-eye gravy and canned vegetables from family gardens. "Deedra's been telling us about your time up in the far north. I was surprised to find out the Canadians speak French. I always thought they spoke English like we do."

"You're right. Most Canadians do speak English as a first language. Quebec's a little different because they began as a French settlement."

Buck turned to Sean. "Do you speak French?"

Sean's fork halted with a portion of ham he had just speared from his plate. "A lot in school. Sometimes with the kids in the neighborhood. But usually English."

"You and your sister have lived in a lot of different places." He turned toward Deedee. "Do you speak other languages?"

"A little. We have to speak French because some of our friends don't speak English very well."

"How do you say *hello* in French?"

"*Comment allez vous?*"

"Sounds pretty from you."

"French is kind of pretty," Deedee said.

Buck turned to Mark. "Do you think we can trust this new Soviet guy—Gorbachev? He seems a little bit nicer than the other leaders they've had."

Apparently, Mark, by virtue of his job, was considered an expert in reading the Soviet mind. "I think Reagan and Gorbachev have hit it off. They actually seem to like each other."

Buck turned to Deedra. "What do you think are the chances we can bring our troops home and not spend so much of our tax money on these foreign shindigs?"

Deedra put down her fork and joined her fingers over her plate, taking time to consider Buck's question. "I have been impressed with how hard our diplomats and generals are trying to bring about a world where we don't need so many soldiers overseas. I think my husband would be pleased with the progress our leaders are making."

Heads nodded, and the conversation strolled down other paths. Mark had a sudden thought of Clair, also no doubt carrying on talks with her family. Maybe in French. Trying to decide where to live.

"Mark," Buck said, "we'd love to have you and your family come back here to live. I'd build you a home myself. All you'd have to pay for is materials."

"That's generous of you. I'll give it some thought. But I do enjoy my career."

"No reason to decide now. The offer's there whenever you want to consider it."

Mark thanked him and drifted into a quandary. These people were part of the vast multitude upholding the country. They were the people he served. But did he still belong in Mocking Bird, Georgia? And how did his children figure in?

"You and Jeremy always were close," Buck said. "He's become a fine man. Done things with his dad's place, and he's really gotten involved with the church."

Mark thought back to the numerous times Jeremy was at Mark's place and the scant number of times Mark had met with his friend at his house, an austere place, too large for an only child and his father. Some of Jeremy's purposeful adulthood was Drayton Pacer's doing, as he was a bit of a father figure for Jer.

That night in his motel room, with the children sleeping in the double bed beside his, he wrestled with thoughts of the future. A home here for his later years? Maybe. But he might have miles to go before that happened—if it ever did. He didn't want to stay with the Foreign Service for a long time, did he?

He had to have purpose. That's why he'd left Mocking Bird.

He would always be a son of this place, but he would never quite belong here because he had a job little understood by his kin and childhood friends.

Regardless, he would always be afflicted with that Southerner's far-from-home yearning—never quite belonging elsewhere either. The taciturn Scotch/Irish from his mother's side and the English from his father's people, plus that pinch of Native American, had melded into an Appalachian identity.

He thought of Montreal, so far from here. Was some anarchist group forming there even now? According to what he'd heard today, the movement had even touched the hills of his childhood home.

Just when hope beckoned with signs of a Cold War thaw, did some other danger threaten, rising to take its place?

CHAPTER TWENTY-TWO

After sleeping late, Mark, Deedra, and the twins feasted at the motel's breakfast bar just before it closed for the day. Mark reined in the twins' temptation for a mostly sugar diet. "Only one sweet thing. Choose between cereal or pancakes or donuts. Not all of them."

"But we don't get to do this very often," Sean argued.

"Pick one."

Sean opted for the donuts. Deedee chose waffles with a lake of syrup.

Deedra said she was going to rest this morning. One of her childhood friends was going to stop by in the afternoon and pick her up for a picnic with her family at one of the parks. Then she and the friend would hash out old times over a meal in one of the fancy new restaurants with a few other women she had known growing up.

Mark and the twins finished the morning with a time of quiet reading in the lobby. Mark caught up on news with the free paper supplied by the motel while the twins read their new novels.

The televangelist Jim Bakker, the newspaper informed Mark, had been indicted for fraud. From another article he discovered that the new US embassy in Moscow would be torn down because Soviet listening devices had been found in the walls. He sighed and turned to the comics.

As the afternoon began, well fortified by their big breakfast, Mark and the twins left to meet Jeremy and his daughters at his downtown store before spending the rest of the day with his friend's family at their house, including supper.

Yes, he could get used to this.

• • • • •

Mark parked in the lot behind Jeremy's store and wandered inside with the kids. Jer sauntered out from an office. "Glad you made it. I wanted you to see the old store—at least, what's left from our time."

Jer made it sound like they were doddering old men.

"I see you've dropped the word *Seed* from your store's name," Mark observed. "Just *Hardware* now."

Jer nodded. "We still carry seed and gardening supplies, of course. Fact is, I only make a small profit on the downtown store—not near as well as the one in the mall. But I have a loyal clientele for the old one. Guess I keep it for old times' sake too. Nowadays, selling housewares and appliances is the way to go. We 're getting so many new households here. Richer old folks, mainly, and some vacation homes. They're going all out for stuff for their houses and yards."

Belle and Janelle appeared from the office area.

Deedee turned toward them. "Do you work here?"

Belle smiled. "Not yet. Someday I might, part time maybe, to earn money for college. Janelle and I came over after school. We only have half day today. Daddy said y'all might come by."

Sean exchanged greetings with the sisters. He appeared to have overcome his shyness, though Mark recognized in his quieter manner the continuing signs of what in his day was called a crush.

"Let's check the toy section," Belle suggested, and they disappeared around a counter of paint displays.

Jer showed Mark around the store before they settled in his office and talked about what various classmates were doing now.

"How do you like the old place?" Jer asked Mark.

"You've gone all modern," Mark answered.

"You should see the mall store. Stop by and see it on your way over tonight."

Mark shook his head. "I like this one."

"Know what you mean."

"Guess we should be moseying back to the motel to freshen up."

Mark tried to separate the twins from the game the four children had begun in the back of the store, but they didn't want to stop. "Tell you what. Why don't I buy the game for you for tonight?"

"No need," Janelle said. "We got it at home."

It ended, of course, with Jeremy making a gift of the game. The twins, properly raised, expressed thanks for his generosity.

"Bunch of great kids, all of 'em," Jer whispered to Mark on their way out. "We done good."

He couldn't argue with that.

• • • • •

Jeremy and Lee Ann's home was a Cape Cod style blended into a hilly background of maple and pine trees. Beds of rhododendron and azalea and other flowers his mother used to grow outlined the house, no doubt Lee Ann's doing.

Jeremy and Lee Ann seem to enjoy the traditional breadwinner/homemaker relationship. Though, Mark learned, Lee Ann did the bookkeeping for Jer's business, having earned a degree in accounting.

In their childhood, Jeremy had been the son of a successful businessman, living in a big white frame house on Main Street—eventually sold to become an upscale townhome. Their friendship had eclipsed class differences, not even noticed by the two boys at the time. Now both were comfortably settled in the American middle class, though in vastly different careers and geographic locations.

Mark pondered again the trade he'd made—a comfortable small-town existence exchanged for a career requiring frequent moves to different countries and cultures, constantly changing. How would his children adjust to adulthood after being dragged around the world in the wake of their father's career?

At the moment, the twins seemed as oblivious to any family differences as their fathers had.

Belle, three years older than the twins, had the innate ability to organize the younger ones without their knowing they were being organized. Deedee appeared to enjoy her relationship with Belle as she might with an older sister.

And why not? His children had missed the large family relationships that even Mark, an only child, had known growing up in Mocking Bird.

Sean had lost his shyness, but he remained quieter than usual, the only boy in the group.

Under Belle's direction they chose games and kept out of the grown-ups' way during supper preparation. Belle left the younger ones from time to time to help her mother with the meal, another tradition Mark remembered from childhood.

As in Buck's house the night before, no before-dinner drinks were served. Jer had apparently kept the nonalcoholic tradition they were raised with. No need for Mark to explain his reasons for not drinking here.

Jer took Mark to a second-floor room that he unlocked with a key he kept on a ring in his pocket. In the room were a couple of gun cabinets, also locked. Jer showed Mark his collection of rifles and pistols.

"I hunt occasionally, but my main interest is shooting competitions." He pointed to certificates on the wall and trophies on shelves. "Neither of my daughters is too interested in guns. Maybe someday I'll have some grandsons to shoot with."

The evening meal was like one his mother might have cooked: fried chicken, mashed potatoes, green beans with cooked onions, and iced tea, all served on a sky-blue linen tablecloth. With thick paper napkins.

After supper, everyone settled in the den with coffee and soft drinks and cherry pie. Jeremy lit a fire in the fancy, glass-enclosed fireplace, unintentionally dividing the group into those young enough to enjoy stretching on the floor beside it and those preferring more comfortable seating.

After the dessert, while the grown-ups talked, the sisters took Deedee and Sean to explore the house and yard. They returned to the den to continue playing from a cornucopia of games and gadgets, no doubt from Jeremy's store. They crouched and stretched and talked and played and laughed often. Sometimes Lee Ann, the most agile of the adults, joined the children in a game, seeming to understand the need for her husband and his best friend to catch up on their lives.

Mark stirred milk and honey into a second cup of coffee. "How come we became friends when our families were so different?"

"After Mama died, my dad insisted I go to church. I think he felt guilty that he was a pagan, but he wanted to honor her that way. It just happened to be the church you and your folks were in."

"My parents took me there every Sunday."

"The church was about as attractive to me as a polecat, but your parents meant the world to me. Your daddy and I got pretty close in those few months before he passed."

"I'm glad." And he *was*, now.

"One of the things he said to me that I remember to this day is that you shouldn't ought to ever stop growing and learning new things. After you went to the Middle East, he read everything he could find about the place. He helped me understand it too. Lots of things I'd never thought about. Neither one of us ever got to go there, but he taught me that you were less likely to hate folks if you learned about them first."

He took a sip of his coffee. "I'm glad you're helping people from different countries get to know each other."

"I am too."

"Do you ever wish you'd stayed here?"

Mark scoffed. "What would I have done if I'd stayed?"

Jer pondered a minute. "With your schooling, you might have taught, maybe at the university."

He considered that. "Some Foreign Service officers do teach after they retire."

"Think you might do that when it's your turn?"

A sense of conviction broke through. "I don't think I can quit yet. I have a feeling something is going to happen in the world that I need to be part of." He would continue for a while yet in the career for which he had left Mocking Bird, even though it meant his children growing up in foreign lands.

He wished he knew how Clair was faring in her trip back to her childhood home. What things drew her there? How attached was she to California?

CHAPTER TWENTY-THREE

*M*ark found Sean unusually quiet as they finished their last breakfast in the motel and loaded up the car. His son rode in the passenger seat as he drove through the old part of town.

Sean sighed as they passed the old hardware store. "Janelle and I talked a lot last night."

"You did?"

"Yeah. She reads a lot, like I do. We both like books about people in different countries. She said she thinks it's great how we get to live all over the world and learn different languages. She'd like to have a job like yours someday. We talked about what we want to study in college. I told her what kinds of things you studied in school—languages and history and foreign affairs."

Mark's homecoming wasn't merely a touching base for him. Processes had been set in motion for others as well. Who could predict the results?

On the highway, Sean glanced back at his grandmother and sister, one dozing and the other lost in a book. "Janelle and I talked some more while Belle and Deedee were looking at stuff in Belle's room and I helped her clear up dishes and take out the garbage. Sometimes Janelle doesn't like Mocking Bird all that much. She feels kind of different. I mean, she and Belle get along, but Belle just wants to get married and teach in Mocking Bird."

"I see." Mark had experienced some of those feelings of not belonging when he was growing up, but he had Jeremy's unstinting friendship to alleviate them.

Mark hadn't assumed he would attend college after high school, knowing the state of his parents' finances. Although they encouraged him to apply for scholarships.

"We're kind of thinking we might go to the same college," Sean continued.

What sorts of forces had been set in motion by this visit?

When Deedee came to a stopping place in her book, she added her own information about Jeremy's daughters. "We're going to write letters after we get back. When we're grown up, Belle said she'll visit the three of us when we work overseas, during summer vacation when she's off."

"Sounds like you all have things planned out very nicely."

How would Jeremy react if his youngest daughter chose a foreign affairs career, taking her out of Mocking Bird? All right for your childhood friend, perhaps, but different for your daughter.

The road turned curvy as they climbed through the mountains, so Mark concentrated on his driving.

CHAPTER TWENTY-FOUR

*M*ark's thoughts wandered during a meeting with Olivier St. Arnoud and the other Canadian officials. A couple of weeks after returning to work his mind was still in vacation mode. The subject of the meeting—the still unsolved mystery of Bill Bancroft's death—contributed to his gloom. Also, the long Christmas season was coming up and Clair wasn't due to return until afterward.

"We can find no trace of this Rooney Steiger," one of the officials said. "No evidence that he has crossed into Canada."

"Which means nothing," St. Arnoud responded. "He uses a fake passport. And with our famous open border, we don't check passports unless something arouses our suspicions."

One of the other attendees shrugged. "He could have sneaked in."

Like many official meetings, it ended with no new conclusions, only verifying what they already knew. An American with Canadian landed immigrant status had apparently been targeted for a killing, possibly related to past activities in the States. Activities related to the dislocations of the sixties and seventies, when groups of young people and a few older adults staged forms of civil disobedience.

But this killing had the earmarks of a personal vendetta.

After the meeting, St. Arnoud confronted Mark over coffee and pastries in a nearby sweet shop. "I find it difficult to believe that Clair Bancroft isn't more involved. Are you sure you aren't missing something?

Something in the past? I'm sure she knows more than she's telling either one of us."

Mark felt himself in the crosshairs. "Despite my friendship with her, I don't know any more than you do. She may be holding back vital information, but if so, I don't know what it is or the reason."

"Come on, Mark. You can be frank with me. Is there something more than friendship between the two of you?"

"We're not having an affair. I have young kids."

Olivier smirked. "Plenty of fathers—and mothers, too, for that matter—have liaisons."

"Well, this one is not. Besides, she's recently widowed."

"After living apart from her husband for a while."

"I admit, I am attracted to her. But it's . . . complicated."

"These things often are."

"If we did get serious, there's my career to think about."

"She isn't attracted to the idea of living all over the globe?"

"I have no idea how she'd feel about it. I haven't asked her."

"Well, something connects her with the murderer of her husband. An affair maybe. Or past crimes related to the anarchist leanings of this group? Treason even? Is she protecting someone?"

Mark wished he knew.

CHAPTER TWENTY-FIVE

Snow had fallen several times since winter's onset, but in manageable amounts. Given the strong possibility of a winter storm in Mark's current assignment, Melba chose to fly into Montreal instead of drive. The family met her at the airport a week before Christmas, dodging busy crowds transiting through the terminal.

The twins knew better than to question Grandmom Melba about presents when meeting her at the airport. Still, Sean couldn't help asking if she was sure her one suitcase was all she had.

"Of course," she said as they loaded it into the Voyager. "I've already taken care of Christmas. I ordered things that Grandmom Deedra has kindly taken care of for me. Much simpler that way. And I didn't have to declare them at customs."

Mark's solemnness definitely lightened after Melba's arrival, with holiday cooking and the crackle of gift wrapping behind closed doors.

• • • • •

Why did tragedies and wrongdoings so often happen around holidays? Or did it just seem that way?

Four days before Christmas, Mike Putnam, the consul general, called all the staff, American and Canadian, to a hurried meeting. A somber announcement dashed the usual jocularity. A plane had crashed over a little town called Lockerbie in Scotland.

"Terrorism of the worst sort," Mike said. "A bomb exploded on the plane. Killed everyone on board and eleven people on the ground."

Mark sucked in his breath, thinking of Melba's recent arrival through an airport, as well as millions of others traveling for Christmas. No doubt the terrorists knew that the added horror of such carnage around a holiday celebrated throughout the Western world would heighten the reaction.

At least one Canadian had been identified among the victims of the Lockerbie bombing. Many of the passengers were Americans returning home for Christmas, including at least two US diplomats. Every American officer in the room, Mark knew, would be searching the casualty lists, wondering if someone they had worked with might have been on that plane.

Mark turned toward the window. Years ago, he had sent his family back to the States one Christmas. And now he insisted on continuing this career that took his family regularly away from the safety of Forest Plains, Missouri, and Mocking Bird, Georgia.

CHAPTER TWENTY-SIX

The Christmas Eve service at church, usually so festive, was a somber affair. Yet, as John reminded his flock, their mood this year was perhaps closer to that first Christmas.

"Mary and Joseph lived in a land occupied by their enemies. They were forced by their conquerors to travel for the purposes of a census, a reminder of the taxes they had to pay those conquerors. Later, Mary and Joseph fled for their lives to a strange country while innocent children were slaughtered. In the midst of our mourning for those killed over Scotland, perhaps we are closer to Christmas than we know."

Upon returning home, Mark and his family drank hot chocolate. Santa had long ago been relegated to a pleasant folk tale, of course, but the children traditionally opened one present before going to bed. Deedee and Sean chose to forgo that tradition this time. They understood, more than most American children their age, that the world could be dangerous.

But perhaps Christmas gained a deeper meaning this year.

When they awoke on Christmas morning, they assembled in the living room in pajamas and robes and stood before the tree. Mark turned on the tree lights, including the angel figure on top.

Melba read the Christmas story from the New Testament book of Luke, in the King James version. "It came to pass in those days, that there went out a decree from Caesar Augustus, that all the world should be taxed . . .

"And she brought forth her firstborn son . . .

"For unto you is born this day in the city of David a Saviour, which is Christ the Lord."

Then, unlike Christmases past, they opened their presents slowly while eating breakfast on trays in the living room.

In the midst of this unusual keeping of the holiday, some of the season's joy returned.

· · · · ·

Melba's flight to Missouri was scheduled after the twins went back to school. Mark and the children said goodbyes at breakfast before they left for work and classes.

Deedra and Melba sat together in the airport lounge before Melba entered the departure area. "I'm so glad you were with us for Christmas this year," Deedra said. "We always want to be together for the holidays, but this one . . . well, you know."

Melba gazed at the crowd that had to board more slowly than usual due to stricter checks put in place by the bombing. "We can face anything together," she said. They'd already seen a Christmas where bombs wiped out relatives merely traveling to be with their families.

"I know," Deedra said. "But it's still downright terrifying."

The loudspeaker droned with announcements about passengers needing to contact airlines officials for rerouted flights.

Deedra moved slightly as someone passed with a monster suitcase. "Mark's vocation doesn't make it easier. His father saw it as the calling he'd always prayed for Mark to find. But I suppose life wouldn't have been easy if he were a missionary, either."

"Deedra," Melba asked, changing the subject, "I forgot to ask. What happened with your post-cancer checkups?"

Deedra's expression perked up. "Thanks to the good Lord, they all showed no evidence of any returning cancer. I'm so thankful. In the midst of all the sorrow in the world, I've been truly blessed. Sometimes I wonder why."

"Probably because you've still got blessings to share."

CHAPTER TWENTY-SEVEN

*C*lair called Mark at work. "I'm back."

He felt a thrill reminiscent of those early days of his Foreign Service career, shortly after he and Reye first met. "How was your visit home?"

"Marvelous. Returning to Montreal at the beginning of winter is a bit of a comedown."

His glance out the window revealed the sunset. "Why don't we meet for supper somewhere, and you can tell me all about it."

"I'd like that. I want to know what happened on your holiday wanderings too."

He called home to say he'd be missing the evening meal with the family in order to eat out with Clair.

"Enjoy your evening out," his mother said. "The twins want to watch *The Princess Bride* tonight. I hope it's not too scary for them."

"Not to worry. Have you seen the book Deedee's reading on the French Revolution? I'm sure the movie can't compare with the horror of cutting off the heads of royalty."

Mark struggled to concentrate as he finished the day's tasks.

He and Clair met in a cozy restaurant, where they piled salad and entrees onto their plates from a buffet.

"Sounds like you're not a fan of participating in Montreal's winter sports—ice skating and skiing and all that," Mark said after they were settled at a table.

"After a California autumn?" Clair chuckled. "What do you think?"

He grinned. "How was your family?"

She focused on her food. "It was great being with them again."

Mark sensed a slight hesitation. "Is Montreal going to lose you to the lower forty-eight?" He almost held his breath waiting for her answer.

She faced him straight on. "My lease isn't up until June, and I certainly don't want to move in the middle of winter. But, yes, I need to move closer to my family. It's time."

So she'd stay through the spring, at least. He took some comfort in that.

"I think in a few months I'll be ready to inventory and close out Bill's bookstore. Before I left for California, I negotiated the lease on it to last till the end of May, a month before my apartment lease ends. Bill loved that store. Whenever I went into it after he died, I could barely glance at all those books."

"The couple next door is still looking after it?"

Clair shook her head. "I hired a student full time to keep it open during the week. She's finished her classes at the university and needs a quiet place to work on her thesis. She was a regular customer of the store."

"So you think you'll keep it open through the spring?"

"I think I'll be ready to begin inventorying sometime in May. Maybe you'll be able to help me go through the books for an end-of-business sale. I could sure use your help."

"Of course." He'd do anything for her. If he could.

CHAPTER TWENTY-EIGHT

*M*ark's courtship with Clair wasn't the falling-in-love kind Mark had known with Reye. It was a slowly building relationship between two people approaching middle age. In addition to being older, Clair and Mark were from very different backgrounds.

He thought about introducing the twins to Clair but put it off. He wasn't sure what he was waiting for. But the timing didn't seem right.

Mark recalled the warning Olivier St. Arnoud had given him.

Bill Bancroft's murderer had not been identified or located. Surely it was somebody Bancroft had angered in those long-ago years of youthful rebellion. And whoever it was had to have gone back to the States by now.

He and Clair fell into an easy routine, normally meeting once during the weekend for an evening meal in the buffet restaurant and sometimes talking until the cleanup crew began putting the food away. By mutual consent, they left in separate cars to return home. He rarely visited her apartment, sensitive to Clair's desire to honor a grieving period for Bill.

They talked often by phone during the week, sharing small incidents in their everyday lives.

Current events stories found their way into their conversations. One night they discussed news out of the central European country of Poland. It had been a satellite country of the Soviet Union, but now the Polish people appeared to be moving toward some kind of democratic change. A labor union called Solidarity had become a political force, leading to free elections.

An author named Salman Rushdie had published a book having to do with a part of the Muslim Quran. *The Satanic Verses* was considered blasphemous by some Muslims, and the leader of Iran put out a *fatwa* against the author, who went into hiding.

An oil tanker had run aground in Alaska and spilled its oil, polluting a wide area of pristine wilderness. The Soviets had called it quits and left Afghanistan. Students in China had begun demonstrating for more democracy. Events were building toward some kind of climax in world affairs. But in Mark's mind, they were always overlaid by his personal relationship with Clair.

The change from bitter cold to bits of spring forcing itself in would have seemed endless, except that each reminder of spring was also a reminder of decisions Mark must make.

Was he ever going to introduce the twins and his mother to Clair? Why was he delaying?

All right. As soon as the weather improved, he would make it happen.

CHAPTER TWENTY-NINE

*M*ark decided to introduce the twins to Clair by way of a bike ride on the path beside the St. Lawrence River after the warmer weather settled in.

"You know," he said one night at supper, "there's an American woman I've been helping. Her husband was killed in a car crash."

"The one you've been dating, right?" Deedee said, regarding her father with a questioning look.

"I guess you'd call it that."

"You're not going to marry her before we even meet her, are you?" Sean asked.

Mark sighed. "Right now, I'm not planning to marry her at all. She's still getting over her husband's death. We're becoming friends, though. So I'd like you to meet her."

"Sounds like a good idea to me," Sean said.

Was that a bit of sarcasm?

The twins had turned eight years old last month. They were still exchanging letters with Jeremy's daughters. The relationships hadn't died off, like he thought they might. He supposed his children were old enough now to have deeper friendships.

He had read in a news magazine article that computer experts had developed a way to communicate through computers. The new tools would allow much quicker correspondence than letters.

What was the world coming to?

• • • • •

Mark was surprised at how deftly Clair put his children at ease. She seemed to have a knack for it, no doubt stemming from her dedication to children's education.

He and the twins had bicycled to her apartment on side streets. Since her apartment was close to the pathway beside the St. Lawrence, they planned to bike together from there.

Clair answered the doorbell and invited them all into the apartment. "How about a bit of breakfast first?" She shepherded them to the small kitchen. The mouth-watering aroma wafting through the apartment originated from a plate of muffins, still warm from the oven. "Please help yourself to muffins and whatever spreads you like." She waved her hand toward the butter and a couple of cheeses.

Perhaps the way to a child's heart was the same as for a man: through their stomachs.

"These muffins are really good, Ms. Bancroft," Deedee said. "They're just-right sweet."

"Thank you, Deedee," Clair answered.

"I like this cheese stuff," Sean said. "Maybe you could give Dad the recipe."

Once out the door, with more food carried in bike baskets, they began a trek down the river, past old factories, some converted into trendy apartments, then through stretches of parks. The day warmed, as did their conversation as they stopped occasionally to rest.

Somewhere along the way, the twins began speaking French to Clair, who responded in the same language.

"You speak it the way some of the kids at school do," Sean said in English. "You must be Quebecois."

"Actually, I'm American. California born and bred."

"But you live here," Deedee said.

"For now. But soon I'll be going back home. Montreal is a lovely place, but I grew up in California."

The kids concentrated on a curvy stretch of the bikeway.

Mark felt a deadening in the pit of his stomach. The sweetness of the day had passed quickly.

CHAPTER THIRTY

*C*lair delivered a tough blow when she called Mark in the middle of the week. "I just received a phone call. When I answered, all I heard was silence on the other end. Then whoever it was hung up."

"They didn't threaten you?"

"No. Probably was just a wrong number. But that's the second time this week."

"Have you told the police?"

"No. I feel foolish."

"I think you should."

"Okay." She agreed. "I'm thinking about going through the bookstore this Saturday and preparing for a close-of-business sale."

It shouldn't have hit him so hard. Had he been expecting a miracle to occur that meant she'd stay?

He seized what could be his last chance to continue their relationship. "I'll be glad to help. Meet you there around ten?"

"Wonderful. I just don't think I can do this final goodbye to Bill alone."

That was what he'd wanted, right? To help get her past her grieving?

• • • • •

On a quiet Saturday morning, Mark and Clair began sorting through the inventory of the tiny bookstore Bill Bancroft had operated, in preparation for the going-out-of-business sale, which would be overseen by the student who had operated the bookstore for Clair during the week. Whatever didn't sell, she had said, she'd take to recycling.

A few other small businesses in this older section of the city dotted a mostly deserted street. In early afternoon, the small repair shop next door closed, followed shortly thereafter by the few others open on weekends.

Mark paused in his work to read a few paragraphs of a translation of meditations by Marcus Aurelius, the Roman philosopher/emperor. Stopping to scan various books had slowed a job requiring a few hours to one taking most of the day. But he couldn't hold back his curiosity.

"Bill ran this bookstore because he wanted to be around books," Clair said, organizing another shelf of reading material. "He didn't care about the money. He liked introducing people to books that fit them."

Mark tore himself away from the book and put it in a box. "Once this is done, I guess there won't be anything left to keep you in Montreal."

She sighed. "Montreal is fine. But California is home."

A sense of loss struck him. Of course, he wasn't going to stay in Montreal, either. His career forever took him to places that weren't home.

He changed the subject. "You and Bill left California because you feared some kind of reprisal from the anarchists. It appears the reprisal came anyway."

"Well, if Bill wasn't safe here, I obviously won't be either. But if I'm going to face danger, I'd prefer being close to family."

Despite youthful rebellion, she had remained close to her parents. So had he. But his family didn't stop him from pursuing the vocation that called him.

"Are the police still keeping an eye on you?"

"They check in occasionally. They told me they pay special attention to my neighborhood on their regular patrols. But I think they've concluded those people were just interested in Bill."

"And do they know why? Vengeance, maybe, because in their way of looking at things, he ran out on them?"

She idly leafed through a book, not looking up at Mark. "He knew things about Rooney and some others."

Something connected her with the murderer of her husband. Past crimes related to this anarchist group perhaps? Was she protecting someone? Surely, there was more that she hadn't revealed.

Giving up on penetrating that solid reserve of hers, Mark helped with the last sorting of books.

As they were leaving, Clair was about to lock the door when she paused. "I forgot to take the money in the cash box." She pushed the door to reenter.

At that second, a bullet whined into the store's interior, barely missing Clair. It thudded somewhere inside. She screamed.

Mark instinctively pushed her ahead of him into the store. He slammed the door behind them and forced her to the floor, then pushed the bolt closed.

A second bullet shattered a glass pane on the door. Mark half dragged Clair behind the counter. "Are you hurt?"

"I don't think so. Are you okay?"

"Yes."

Another bullet shattered a second pane of glass.

Mark grabbed the telephone off the counter and made a call.

Two additional bullets smashed through the glass panes. On the floor behind the counter, Mark wrapped his arm around Clair and pulled her tightly to him.

Sirens sounded. Relief flooded Mark.

An unmarked vehicle took the two of them to the police station.

Despite the tension of the situation, Mark caught Olivier's barely concealed I-told-you-so smirk as he led them to his office for a question-and-answer session. Mark and Clair provided what little information they could.

St. Arnoud spoke mostly to Clair, in French. Although Mark's French was adequate, he sensed a comradery between them not available to him.

The shooter had fled the scene, but he was seen throwing away his gun. The gun was recovered and would no doubt be tied to Rooney Steiger by his fingerprints.

They discovered the place where Rooney had stayed during his trips and the false passport he'd used. They even found the car that killed Bill there, hidden in a garage.

St. Arnoud allowed Mark to call the operations center at the State Department office. He assured the duty officer he would file a report explaining the series of events—even though he certainly didn't have all the answers yet.

He phoned home, letting his mother know that he was caught up in a "consulate emergency" and might be getting in quite late. He had to settle his nerves before he walked in the door of his house.

CHAPTER THIRTY-ONE

*M*ark sat on Clair's couch, drinking the hot tea she insisted would calm them down. He put his arm around her shoulder and pulled her close. "Tell me more about Rooney."

She knitted her hands together. What was she hiding? Was she afraid Mark would no longer accept her because of her past relationships? Surely she knew better now.

"There's a lot I haven't told you or the police. You see, I was protecting Bill by separating from him."

She sat up, loosening herself from his arm. "Rooney had a crush on me. He was very jealous of Bill. In the beginning of our relationship, we tried to hide from him how serious we were."

"So his murder wasn't about a fight between different factions of Rooney's group?"

"It was, yes. But jealousy was at the root of it."

"How do you think he found you at the bookstore?"

Clair looked at her hands. "I suppose he just searched around for bookstores, knowing he'd eventually find Bill either running one or as a steady customer."

"Why didn't you tell the authorities that? They would have provided more protection for you."

"It's okay now. They'll catch Rooney. And he'll be convicted of premeditated murder. He'll be in prison a long time. He won't bother me again."

Mark grimaced as he realized he would have to visit this man in jail, part of his job as an American consular officer.

No, he'd let Joyce, his junior officer, visit Rooney. Good training for her. Although a Canadian jail wouldn't begin to prepare her for visiting the prisons in other countries where she might serve. Too bad Rooney Steiger wouldn't end up in one of them.

Mark looked at his watch. Church would be starting in a few hours. "My family will be wondering what happened to me."

"Of course."

They stood.

"I'll give you a call tomorrow afternoon, okay?"

"That would be nice. I may visit that Friends' group in the morning." He hoped she could find comfort there.

• • • • •

After about four hours sleep, Mark struggled out of bed to call Mike Putnam. The consul general had just brought in the newspaper but hadn't opened it. Mark briefed him about the publicity that might descend on the consulate as a result of Rooney's attempted killing.

The CG uttered a short curse. A rustling of papers told Mark the story wasn't on page one.

"Well," Mike finally said, "it's not too bad. You're identified as a customer who happened to be in the store when Steiger attempted to kill a former girlfriend, a Canadian citizen with joint American citizenship. Says they knew each other in California."

Bless Olivier for tagging him as a customer.

"Must have been pretty terrifying. Says here you and Clair managed to hide until the police came. Fortunate. You've notified the department, I assume."

"Yes." Mark sighed. "But you need to know, Clair is a friend of mine."

"Casual friend? Or more?"

"We're just friends." He hoped Rooney Steiger would not realize his close relationship with Clair and drag him into the picture. If he was searching for Clair at the bookstore, he probably didn't know where she lived.

"OK. Why don't you give our public affairs people a heads-up."

"Will do."

Mark sent the family on to church, then called the consulate's public affairs officer. Then he called Joyce Minnick, the junior consular officer, to brief her on their new American prisoner and task her with visiting Steiger—this afternoon, if possible.

"I don't blame you for not wanting to see him. He almost killed you! If it were me, I'd have to be restrained from retaliating."

Restraint indeed.

On Monday afternoon, Mark read Joyce's report, which altered his perception of Rooney. From his own brief interaction with the man, Mark had thought him to be a blubbering idiot. Joyce wrote: "He had a glare of pure hatred. Didn't try to defend himself. Said Bancroft and his wife deserved to die for what they'd done to him, though he was vague about what that was. Frankly, I think he's insane."

Yes, insane with the kind of hatred, and megalomania, that dictators suffered from, leading to atrocities like Stalin's crimes in Ukraine.

That evening, Mark stopped by Clair's apartment to fill her in on Joyce's report of the man who had tried to kill them. She pressed her lips together, probably to prevent her emotions from spilling out.

"You're going to have to testify against him." He would have to give testimony also. Hopefully, he could do it in a private setting. He'd have to ask the Department for advice. "The consulate keeps a list of local lawyers for any American who thinks they need one."

"I have an appointment tomorrow with a lawyer. My brother got a recommendation from a friend of our family who lives here."

"Even better."

CHAPTER THIRTY-TWO

"What's that?" Clair asked, nodding at the briefcase Mark carried into her apartment on Friday night. They'd planned to share a meal there, just the two of them. The twins had been invited to a friend's house. Deedra said she was looking forward to a quiet evening at home, with full access to the television.

"I'll share it with you after dinner." Mark inhaled deeply. "The aroma of your food makes it impossible for me to think of anything else right now."

After a delicious shepherd's pie, followed by a cake liberally seasoned with Quebec's traditional maple syrup, Mark pulled out papers from the briefcase. "Bid cables for my next assignment list," he informed her.

"Next assignment?"

"Diplomats in the US State Department's foreign service change assignments every two or three years."

"Oh." Her eyes closed as if a sudden understanding had come to her. The expression that passed across her face was sheer pain.

"What is it, Clair?"

She stood and walked into the bedroom. Dread crept into his soul. She returned with a small metal box and sat down, the box on her lap.

She opened the box, filled with photos. She pulled out the top one, stared at it a moment, and handed it to Mark.

A boy, about four, grinned. In his eyes, Mark detected a hint of Bill Bancroft's passport picture.

"Who is he?"

Clair set the box on the floor and took the photo from Mark, placing it on her lap to study. "I'm not proud of the way I lived back in the so-called free love era. While I was with Rooney, Bill and I fell for each other. We carried on a secret affair. Until I realized I was pregnant."

"Bill's child?"

"Before he was born, I wasn't sure. When it became obvious I was pregnant, Rooney would assume the child was his. He would try to force me to abort, just like he'd done with other women in our group. He wanted no responsibility for children."

She stared at the picture. "I couldn't stand the idea of that."

Mark remembered the joy he and Reye shared when they found out she was finally pregnant.

"I didn't want any part of the life I was living. I loved Bill, and he loved me, and we wanted to share our lives together."

"What did Bill say about your pregnancy?"

"That he would not let this child be harmed—whether it was his or not."

The son of an unmarried mother of seventeen, Bill would not have wanted any child to be aborted.

"Rooney became furious when he realized I wasn't his any longer. I'm not sure what would have happened if he hadn't been taken in by the authorities for suspicion of damage to public property. While he was in jail, Bill and I had left the group. We stayed with my family. When Christian was born, his features made it obvious who the father was."

"Did you feel safe there?"

"I'd never told Rooney where they lived. But I knew when he found out I'd left him for Bill, his ego wouldn't be able to stand it. We were afraid for our lives, and for the baby too. Rooney wouldn't have any qualms about killing him to get back at us."

132

"What did you do?"

"I gave Christian to my brother and his family to adopt."

Mark couldn't imagine the pain of that sacrifice. "Now that Rooney's out of the way, do you think you'll get him back?"

She shook her head. "My brother and his wife are wonderful parents. I couldn't take Christian from them. As we agreed from the beginning, they started telling Christian about a year ago that their Auntie Clair is really his mom, but when he was born, she couldn't keep him, so we all chose them to be his parents. When he gets older, we'll tell him more about his birth father."

"Did Rooney ever find out you were pregnant?"

"No one knew except my family. To protect Christian, Bill and I told friends we wanted to start a new life in Canada."

"I'm so sorry for what you've been through."

Clair placed the picture on the table. "You understand now why I can't accept any kind of life that would keep me from living close to my son, now that it's safe to do so."

"Of course."

She stared at the window. "You could come with me to California. My family would love you. And your family."

By continuing his career, he would have to give up two homes: his life in Mocking Bird and one with Clair in California. But the call of his career wasn't the only consideration. If Reye had lived as an invalid instead of dying so quickly, he would have given up his career in a heartbeat to take care of her.

But, he realized with stark reality, he wasn't drawn to Clair in that compelling way.

That realization lightened his decision but did nothing for the emptiness in his heart.

CHAPTER THIRTY-THREE

*J*ohn, Mark's friend and pastor, visited him at home when the news broke about the shooting at the bookstore. Mark was grateful for someone to share his unexpected thankfulness to God. But the gravity of what had almost happened still hit him hard at times.

For weeks he had been consumed with carrying out a normal workload while giving testimony in the case against Rooney Steiger. Mike Putnam spoke up for him and persuaded the State Department to provide him with a lawyer to be present for the hearing. The relationship between Mark and Clair was never mentioned. Rooney Steiger must not have known he existed until he saw him with Clair when he tried to kill her.

Mark saw Clair briefly when she returned to Canada to give her testimony. They ate at one of their old hangouts before she went back. Amazingly, he felt relief that they had broken off their relationship. He was both surprised and delighted that he felt no desire to reignite it. Nor, apparently, did she.

The facts were indisputable. Rooney would be locked up, probably for the rest of his life. And Mark would never have to visit him since one of the junior officers could do that.

John called again in late September and suggested a visit on their bench before the weather change drove them indoors for the long winter. Mark gladly accepted. He wanted to congratulate John on his recent announcement about his engagement to one of the congregation's members, a woman Mark didn't know.

"*Mabruk*," Mark said. Noting John's puzzlement, he added, "It's an Arabic expression of congratulations."

John's face returning to its happy aura. "Thanks. I thought I would never marry. God just slips up on you sometimes, bestowing joy when you least expected it."

Mark wished God would see fit to slip up on him like that. But he kept the sour thought to himself. After all, he was alive.

"You have, what, another year here?" John asked. "I'll miss you and our talks."

"As will I." Mark decided to take advantage of John's friendship while he could. "There are some things I'd like to share with you. I assume your priestly role will allow you to keep a secret?"

"Of course." John became suddenly serious.

Mark laughed. "Don't worry. I'm not confessing my sins, though I know I have plenty of them." He told John about Clair and Christian. She had given Mark permission to talk to his minister friend about them before she left.

John's pastoral instinct apparently kicked in. "I hadn't realized what a rough spot you've been in. Though I must say, I think you made the right decision. I truly believe you'll find the woman you need to complete you—someday."

The gloom of the day lifted slightly. "Okay, you've done your priestly duty. I feel only slightly depressed now."

A couple of students passed, their swift walks indicating lateness to a class.

"Seriously," Mark continued, "I do feel relieved. The decision was mutual. We'll remain friends, even though most likely we'll never see each other again."

A blue jay flew past. Then a robin slowly descended, picked something off the sidewalk, then returned to its perch.

"I'll offer special prayers today for you," John said.

"Thanks. You might suggest divine direction for me in this career I've decided to keep. I'll be bidding on a new assignment soon. Have you been keeping up with the news?"

"Yes. I'm happy about what I hear concerning Mikhail Gorbachev and your President Bush. They appear to have developed a rather friendly relationship. Amazing. The leaders of the two main contenders in the world becoming friends."

"No great nuclear world war this time, thank the good Lord."

"We've been given a wonderful gift, a bit of breath for a new beginning," John said. "I wonder how we'll use it."

Mark decided he would bid on a Washington assignment next. And maybe it would happen. If so, they could return to the house in Arlington they had last lived in with Reye.

"Do you think there's a chance for true world peace?"

"Oh, there's definitely a chance. But it will involve more than taming the Cold War."

"Oh?"

"Movements for disorder are always working beneath the surface. We're never free of it. In my profession, we call it temptation and sin."

"You don't sound too excited about this break in the Cold War."

"Oh, I'm very enthusiastic about it. I think it will give us a chance for some good things, no matter how long it lasts. We should always take advantage of a chance to do some good while we have it."

Mark looked away. "Whether I go to Washington or get called back to a foreign post, I'm definitely going to leave here."

John studied him for a moment. "In your true self, you're glad, aren't you?"

"Yes. It's my calling, I guess. The only place that's truly home is wherever I'm serving at the moment."

• • • • •

Back in his office, Mark checked the cables. He lingered over one from the US embassy in Kuwait, a small oil-rich country in the Gulf, north of Saudi Arabia.

Since the long war between Kuwait's neighbors, Iran and Iraq, had ended in a truce, Iraq's leader, Saddam Hussein, was attempting to build up his country's oil fields. Was he eyeing his neighbor to the south?

Mark derided himself for spending so much time following happenings in the Middle East. He was going to bid on Washington assignments next, right?

Still, he reread the cable.

Where would he end up next? God only knew.

ORDER INFORMATION

To order additional copies of this book, please visit
www.redemption-press.com.
Also available at Christian bookstores, Amazon, and Barnes and Noble.

Milton Keynes UK
Ingram Content Group UK Ltd.
UKHW041158040324
438885UK00007B/498